Felix Publishing 2021
email: info.felixpublishing@gmail.com
Print copies available from publisher.

200 Years Before the Mast

Print Edition: ISBN: 978-1-925662-42-9
Digital book release: ISBN: 978-1-925662-43-6

Author: Dr. Peter T. Scott

Registration:
Thorpe-Bowker +61 3 8517 8342
email: bowkerlink@thorpe.com.au

200 Years before the Mast

Dr. Peter T. Scott

Table of Contents

Chapter One

The Experiment

"What ho, Sinclair!" came the jocular greeting as the door to my laboratory burst open and in walked the Right Honourable Algernon FitzAdam. 'Fitzy' as he was known was lanky, had a shock of unruly red hair and was irrepressible in spirit and was well-known about the college as a prankster. He was a particular friend of mine and he was not one to pay attention to the large, red flashing light outside of my laboratory door nor the sign below it which read:

'DANGER – Harmful Radiation'

Fitzy and I had been good friends ever since our undergraduate days. He had followed the path of the historian and did his Honours paper on some obscure aspect of the Royal Navy during the Napoleonic Wars. I had shared his interest in the 'Days of Fighting Sail' as it was a welcome distraction from the even more obscure mathematics and the theoretical physics of my research into the nature of atomic particles.

"How are you Old Fruit?" he said with his usual drawl; he had the habit of calling everybody 'Old fruit'. He was a son of some minor peer near Lowestoft in Sussex and affected a type of speech which I thought was only found in the novels of P. G. Wodehouse.

"Speaking of fruit." He continued, coming around the side of the laboratory to avoid my apparatus. "I managed to filch a pineapple for you from the Dean's table at last night's New Year bash. Saw that you weren't there – missing the end of good old 1995 and all that – and so here I am with my ill-gotten gains."

"Thanks, Fitzy." I replied, turning once more to the console which I had set up in the corner of the laboratory. "Be a good chap and come over here as I am about to fire 'the Beast' up.

I had worked extremely hard for my Doctorate in particle physics and now was a Doctoral Research Fellow looking into the new concept of high-speed tachyons. Fitzy had also started his Doctorate in an even more obscure study of early sailor life in the late eighteenth-century and was still plodding along.

He had christened my apparatus which took up most of the space in my small laboratory 'the Beast' because of its complexity of tubes, metal plates, wires and other paraphernalia which seem to almost fill the room.

I handed him my spare pair of dark glasses which was some protection against any stray reflections from the light of my lasers. He came and stood behind me as I flicked several switches and adjusted knobs on my console.

In theory, I was performing a more sophisticated version of Rutherford's experiment in which the great man had bombarded a very thin sheet of gold foil with alpha particles from a radioactive source. He discovered that most of these particles went right through the foil but that some were slightly deflected and a few bounced back. From this experiment, he deduced that atoms of gold were mostly open space with a small central nucleus.

My research some eighty-four years later was more interested in bombarding the nucleus of the atom in the hope of dislodging some of the smaller and so far theoretical particles it contained. There had been considerable success in some of the major research laboratories in this field in the nineteen sixties and in particular the research paper by Feinberg in 1967 suggesting the possible existence of a high-speed particle which he called a tachyon.

My research was not in the league of these major players, since I was still an unknown and it had been made quite clear to me that I was lucky to get my small closet-like laboratory and the small research grant for my experiments. Only my good relationship with the professor and a well-received Doctoral thesis had got me this far.

My apparatus, like that of Rutherford was relatively simple; two large metal disks as electrodes separated by about a metre with a sheet of lead between them. This had a fine layer of carbon on one side closest to the negative terminal plate which was an annulus really with a circular hole in it through which several rotating beams of argon lasers were fired. My hypothesis was also very simple and perhaps naïve with the hope that the high voltage between these plates would disrupt the electron clouds around the lead atoms which would allow the rotating laser beams to knock off parts of the atoms' nuclei.

Fitzy strolled around the cluttered confusion of wires, tubes and other paraphernalia to where I was standing looking at my console and adjusting the knobs to the primary voltage for the Rühmkorff coil, which would give my secondary, high frequency voltage across the plates of about fifty thousand volts, and the power supply to the four lasers and the motor which would spin then at high speed.

"Looks rather exciting, Old Chap," said Fitzy leaning over my shoulder as he was a good deal taller than I.

"Stay close, Fitzy and put on these dark glasses to stop stray reflections from the lasers" I replied handing him my spare set whilst I quickly put on my own.

"Here we go!" I said and with a dramatic hand movement, threw the main switch that would send the appropriate power to my apparatus giving the expected result. The sensors set at the side of the device would detect any particles thrown off the nuclei and the result would be a few small blips on the straight line on my cathode ray oscilloscope screen which we were now watching with some intensity.

There were no tell-tale blips, only a large flash of blue light from behind us and the sweet, pungent smell of burnt pineapple. We both turned at the same time.

"Oi! Where's my pineapple?" yelled Fitzy, his Wodehouse English forgotten for the moment.

"Where did you put it?" I asked.

"Right there in that space on your bench." He said pointing to the small space between the lead sheet and the positive terminal of my apparatus; the only available bench space in the whole room.

"You great clot, Fitzy!" I shouted. "That was right in the core of my experiment! Ruined!"

"Sorry, Old Fruit, but where is the pineapple or at least its remains?"

Fitzy for once showed some scientific imagination. There was absolutely nothing in the spot where he had put the pineapple. No burnt remains. Nothing.

"That is strange" I pondered and turned the power to the apparatus off. I picked up the long wooden ruler which I kept on my blackboard and carefully poked the space where the pineapple should have been. Nothing.

"Looks like 'The Beast' has devoured my pineapple completely. What?" Fitzy said, having regained his usual way of speaking. "Well! No harm done and it looks like it may be the right time for a pint or two at the old 'Eagle'".

He had that quirk of personality which always saw a way out of any problem or mishap and usually it would involve going to 'The Eagle' – the pub frequented by most students at the university – for 'a pint or two'.

There was nothing more to do as my apparatus seemed to be intact and the space where the pineapple had been place was completely clean; not even a spec of burnt tissue could be seen. I rechecked my dials and switches to make sure that all the power was off and then leaned up and opened the high windows of the laboratory to get rid of the smell of toasted pineapple. I followed Fitzy out of the laboratory, remembering at the last moment to turn off the red hazard warning light and closed and locked the door behind me.

We had more than a few pints at 'The Eagle', Fitzy and I, but it was a good break away from the tedium of my experimental work which had taken over my life in the past few months. Fitzy had got on to his favourite topic, the 'Days of Fighting Sail' and I was an eager listener as I found such a time a fascinating era. Perhaps I had been born much too late, for I felt at home in listening to his stories of some of the great frigate captains of that day. The actions and careers of such men as Pellew, Cockburn, Cochrane and Trevallyn had always been of great interest to me. Having been born and raised near the sea at Wembury near the great port of Plymouth, I had a natural liking for the history of this part of the country.

I left Fitzy as night was beginning to fall and walked back to the college and to my laboratory for, I had remembered that I had left the windows open. Unlocking the door to my laboratory, I walked into to a room still full of the smell of burnt pineapple and there to my surprize was the burnt remains of the fruit sitting on the bench where Fitzy had left it. It was now in the space where there was not even a trace of burnt fruit when we had left the laboratory. How had it suddenly returned?

I sat for a while and looked at the burnt husk of the pineapple sitting incongruently in the middle of my complex apparatus. Fitzy had claimed that he left it on that spot before I started up my latest experiment. Then it was not there and now, several hours later it was! Confusion!

Having a few pints was not conducive for scientific thought, so I decided to start afresh next morning. I closed the windows which I had left open, checked that there was no longer any power to my apparatus, cleaned off the pineapple mess from the bench and left my laboratory, making sure that the door was locked.

It was a false premise to imagine that I would get any sleep that night. With still some alcohol flowing through my brain, I had tossed off my outer garments, put on my pyjamas and fell onto my bed in the small room allocated to me at the college. What little sleep I had was restless and full of images of pineapples suddenly appearing out of nowhere. I awoke in a lather of sweat, got up and stared for a while out of my casement window and across the moonlit lawn of the college's quadrangle. The chimes from the clock in the tower of St Mary's droned out its long cadence then finally got around to chiming out the hour; two in the morning.

I could not sleep anymore, so I picked up my clothes where I had thrown them on the floor and put them on over my pyjamas as the early morning chill was starting to make its presence felt. Down the stairs and across the quadrangle to the colonnades which led to the small alleyway and to my room in the Department of Physics. It was strange walking through the university at night; the eery shadows and moonlight stretching across the empty quadrangle and the dark silence of the alleyways and paths. Luckily, I had been trusted with a set of keys to the Department and so I entered, very much feeling like some felon about to do some mischief. Up the stairs and down the long corridor to my small room. I switched on the light and gave my apparatus a quick inspection. No pineapple this time and only the smell of stale air filled the room. I opened the small windows and switched on the main power to my apparatus. In my fitful sleep, my brain had turned over all of the variables and possibilities of what had happened the previous afternoon.

I had reasoned that the only independent variables in the previous 'experiment' was the choice of a pineapple and the electrical field which I had set up to induce tachyons to be emitted from my target. I had snatched an orange from my dresser hoard of fruit on my way of my room carefully placing it where Fitzy's pineapple had been placed; between the carbonised lead sheet target. Next, I carefully looked at the setting on the dial which controlled the voltage of the primary circuit. I thought that there may be a connection between this value and the amount of time that the pineapple had not been visible. To test my hypothesis, I reduced the voltage by a small amount. Donning my protective glasses, I threw the switch which would power up the rotating bank of lasers to apply the secondary voltage across the main plates. This time I watched the proceedings.

The laser beams formed a twisted coil of light striking the target plate on the opposite side to the orange. There was the usual crackle of high voltage and its accompanying electrical effects around the room. For a while nothing happened; the orange just sat there on the bench. Suddenly there was a brief flash of electrical blue light similar to that observed with a lightning flash, a rancid smell of burnt orange and then there was only vacant space where my orange had been. Astounding!

Now it had been about three hours from the time that Fitzy and I had left for the local pub and the time that I had returned to find the return of the pineapple. How long would it take for my orange to appear? The horrid thought occurred to me that perhaps to keep all of the variables consistent I should have used another pineapple but at such a late hour that was impossible. Besides, knowing

Fitzy, he would have swiped the only pineapple from the Dean's table.

I turned my desk chair around so that I could face my apparatus and sat down for a long wait. There was total silence in the room; no coarse cries from below from students running across the quadrangle late for lectures, only the metallic ticking of the old alarm clock which I kept on my desk.

I was about to fall asleep when I noticed a faint blue glow appearing between my target sheet and the positive terminal of my apparatus where the orange had been placed. Suddenly there was the blue flash of light again and the familiar rancid smell of burnt fruit. My orange had returned, two hours and twenty-two minutes after it had disappeared.

So, my hypothesis was correct! The amount of applied primary voltage determined the amount of time that the subject (the fruit) would disappear and then reappear. But to where?

It was easy to figure out why the fruit had been burnt as the applied secondary voltage would easily do that at any rate. The only question was where did the fruit go? I had cautiously pocked the space from which the fruit had disappeared with a long wooden pole used to close my high windows to see if the fruit had simply become invisible but there had been no resistance. The fruit had gone somewhere, but where? It suddenly occurred to me, looking at my old alarm clock that it was not a question of where, but when! It was somewhat of a shock to me when the realisation came that perhaps the pineapple and my orange and moved forward in time and not space. Had I accidently discovered how to travel in time?

Fitzy did not appreciate my loud knocking on his door at five in the morning and he uttered a string of words which P.G. Wodehouse would never had known. But he opened the door anyway and looked at his visitor through very bloodshot eyes.

"Its some un-Godly hour in the f…… morning, Sinclair! What the hell do you want? Is the college on fire or what?" he said in a mixture of anger and alarm.

"It works, don't you see! I know where your pineapple went!"

"I know what you can do with your pineapple!" he threatened "so what do you want at this hour?"

"I need a witness and you are the only one handy at this hour for the next experiment." I said in rather a sheepish voice. "Do you have any more fruit?"

Fitzy was, even at this hour a good-natured type, so he dressed in a robe; all the while muttering unkind comments about the genealogy of all physicists and grabbed a half-eaten apple from his bedside table.

He followed me back to Department of Physics where I stopped off to snatch up some wire gauze squares from the Undergraduate laboratory.

"A Faraday Cage! That's what was needed to save your pineapple!" I cried and opened the door to my room.

"A what?" he questioned.

"A Faraday Cage!" I cried in some exasperation thinking that even a person like Fitzy would know what that was. "The great inventor of the dynamo,

Michael Faraday showed that even high voltage would not penetrate the interior of a metal mesh cage. He experimented with himself as the subject, but I guess that your poor specimen of an apple will have to do."

I put the gauze squares together to make small cube of wire and placed the apple into its centre before closing down the last wire mesh side. I then place the whole affair into the appropriate place on the bench within my apparatus. This time I readjusted the primary voltage dial to an even lower value and handed Fitzy a pair of safety glasses. I looked at my old alarm clock in the semi darkness and it showed 5:17 am. I threw the main switch.

There was the usual noise of the motors, the bright rope of laser light and then the blue flash. The entire mesh cube and its apple passenger had disappeared but this time there was no rancid smell of burnt fruit. Fitzy looked at me with his mouth open and I motioned him to sit down on my only chair, holding up my index finger to my mouth for silence.

We waited as the light of the early summer morn slowly illuminated my apparatus and the empty space where the Faraday Cage had stood. Silence and waiting.

Suddenly a glow appeared on the bench and once again there was the blue flash. The time now was 6: 24 am; the Faraday Cage once more stood where it had been placed. I turned off the apparatus and waited for a while in case the outer surface of the cage had retained any electrical charge. I touched it carefully with the back of my knuckle and found that it was neither charged nor warm. I opened the top of the cage and pulled out Fitzy's apple.

"There you are, Old Fruit!" I said with some jocularity. "You can finish eating it now."

"Not likely after some 'mad scientist' has been at it. I'll probably turn into some hideous beast if all of the movies are right." He said with a distinct lack of humour. "So, what had you just proven, anyway?"

"I have found a way to send organic matter into the future." I said with some pride.

Fitzy looked up at me in the faint light and shrugged his shoulders. "I'm happy for your discovery

Sinclair, but if you could send the apple back in time then that would interest me. I could do all of my research in real time and not have to ferret around in old bookshops looking for details of sailor life in the eighteenth-century."

With that he wished me a 'good morning' and mumbled something about catching up on some sleep in the extended future and left the room.

What he had said made some sense for a change. If I had been successful in sending an object into the future and if Albert Einstein was correct that time and space were a continuum, then surely, I could send an object back in time. But how?

The early morning is a good time for rational thought. I went through the variables which I had used in my recent experiment and wondered. What would happen if I reversed the polarity of my primary circuit so that the target object would now be between the carbonised lead and the negative terminal of the secondary circuit?

It was a simple matter to reverse the polarity of the primary circuit by a few adjustments to the contacts of the Rühmkorff coil which produced the high voltage to the main secondary plates. I kept the voltage of the primary circuit at the same value of the last experiment and replaced Fitzy's apple into the Faraday Cage and then then replaced it onto the bench between the carbonised lead and the new negative terminal. I stood back, readjusted my safety glasses and threw the switch.

To my joy, there was the usual blue flash and the Faraday Cage disappeared. But to when?

I was now apprehensive. How could I test that my object had gone back in time and not once more into the future? I waited for over two hours, just sitting in the small room as the morning sunlight began to stream through my small upper windows. Nothing happened, so I switched off the apparatus and went downstairs and out into the college to have breakfast at the Refectory. Had my experiment been a success or did the apple and its metal wire box simply disappear into the ether of space-time?

Breakfast was a hurried affair and I quickly went back to my experiment hoping that something would have changed. Then it suddenly occurred to me that even the smartest of minds will often overlook the obvious. My previous experiments had sent the objects into the future where I had eventually caught up with them. Sending an object back in time would not give such an opportunity so Fitzy's apple would have popped up back in the past and most likely when I had been banging on his door at five in the morning. I needed to reverse the settings and try and get the apple back to the current time.

I reasoned that if a simple reversing of the polarity of the primary voltage would send the object back in time, then another reversal back to the original setting would push it forward in time to the present. Accordingly, I reversed the wires coming from the primary source but then added a little extra voltage to make up for the time which had elapsed during breakfast. I set up the apparatus and threw the switch. Nothing.

I sat down dejected but then thought of how imprecise my adjustments had been so I decided to put aside my sense of failure and give it some time. Almost exactly one hour later, there was the glow and then the blue flash and there was my Faraday

Cage and its resident apple back on my bench unharmed. I had been successful in sending an object both back into time and then forward in time to its original position.

Chapter Two

The Time Traveller

So far, my experimentation had been a rather *ad hoc* affair using simple organic subjects, namely fruit. Now I needed to find out if I could send a more complex living organism forward or back in time.

So, the next day, I went downstairs to the preparation room of the Department of Physics to consult its chief technician, Mr. McConachie. He was a Scot of dour appearance and had a reputation of being a 'hard man', especially on students and post-doctoral researchers who always seem to be wanting something. In truth, the Department of Physics could not survive without his unique abilities which usually required the construction of various apparatus made up of spare built parts which would defy the average engineer. In this preparation room and its associated storerooms, McConachie was the absolute power.

I found him bent over his long, wooden workbench tinkering with some complicated electronic device which looked futuristic in its own right. I coughed in an attempt to make my presence known. No reaction, so I tried a more direct approach.

"Good morning, Mr McConachie." I said cheerfully.

The Scot turned and looked at me sternly over his bifocals, raising one dark eyebrow in the process.

"Aye, it is thon, Dr Sinclair. Noo whit is it ye wull be wantin'?"

McConachie was always direct and not one for much social conversation.

"I know it may seem a bit irregular, but I would like a live mouse if you could arrange it?" I said with some trepidation for the request was unusual, even for a research Physicist.

"Ye'll waant a wee moose is it then? Ah kin git ye a muckle rat easy enouch fae th' Department o' Biology, bit ye'll waant a wee moose, ye say?"

"Yes please, Mr. McConachie, if that's not too much trouble. A live one." I replied.

"Ach aye. Ah think that ah kin dae that, bit it wull tak' a tae o' days. Noo ye dinnae wantae be hurting th' wee cratur wull you?" he said with some atypical concern

"It's for a Physics experiment, you see and I don't think that the mouse will come to any harm... I hope." I replied, feeling like a young schoolboy who has just asked his teacher for rare piece of expensive equipment. The old technician gave me another dark look over his bifocals:

"Come back in a tae o' days 'n' ah wull hae yer moose fur ye."

With that, he turned his back and continued tinkering with the unknown electronic gadget on his bench. I'm sure that if one wanted to construct a nuclear reactor or some other exotic piece of equipment, then the innovative Mr. McConachie would have said the same thing, so I quickly left, closing the door quietly behind me.

True to his word, the dependable technician had a small grey mouse within a handmade wooden cage ready for me on the morning of the second day. I thanked him for his efforts and quickly returned to my small laboratory, feeling somewhat akin to my new subject.

I had already set up my apparatus for a forward journey as before with the same voltage setting in the primary so that the mouse would appear again in a little over an hour's time. I carefully took the little mouse out of its cage and placed it in a smaller wooden cage within the mesh cube. I felt a little apprehensive and was full of compassion for the little creature and hoped that my hypothesis for its safety would be correct. I said a silent prayer for small thing, adjusted my goggles and threw the main switch. There was the usual blue flash and the Faraday Cage and its furry occupant disappeared.

The next hour was one of concern and some soul-searching about using a live subject for my experiment. I watched both my battered old alarm clock and the bench space with some foreboding. Exactly one hour and fifteen minutes later there was the welcome blue glow and sudden flash of light and the Faraday Cage reappeared. My small furry companion twitched its nose and looked out at the rest of its strange surroundings. There was a faint blue glow around its body which persisted for a while and so I waited until it dissipated and then took my mouse out of his confinement and put it back into McConachie's larger box. My little traveller seemed to be in good health and was rewarded with some fine Stilton cheese which I had taken from the Dean's table at breakfast.

My little friend, whom I had named Herbert, after that great storey-teller Herbert George Wells, who's novel the *Time Machine* had been an absorbing boyhood read, was given some well-earned rest. Later that afternoon, I repeated the experiment with the polarity set on past time but all other parameters identical and sent him back to a time when I was not in my laboratory. I thought that there would be too much confusion if a mouse in a cage had suddenly appeared in my laboratory before the beginnings of my experiment. I reversed the polarity and returned Herbert to the current time without any apparent side effects except that peculiar blue glow which soon faded. I attributed this phenomenon to some minor static electrical effect.

Having satisfied myself that a living animal could be sent forward and back into time and be returned, I gave Herbert some additional cheese and pumpkin seed as a reward and then took him back to Mr. McConachie so that he could see that there had been 'no hurting th' wee cratur'. I also made a request that Herbert be released where he had been caught. McConachie's reply suggested that Herbert would indeed be rehabilitated to an easy life:

"Och aye, back tae th' comfort o' th' Dean's scullery fur ye." He said, accepting the wooden cage and my small former assistant.

The next few weeks were spent calibrating my apparatus. That is, determining by experimentation what settings of the primary voltage would give the desired time for forward or reverse polarity. I had already established that everything about my apparatus was a constant variable except the polarity of the primary circuit and its voltage. In other words, the length of the travel in time was in direct proportion to the voltage of the primary circuit and that the Faraday Cage was necessary to overcome the effects of the high voltage of the secondary voltage on the Time Traveller. I calibrated the voltage settings of the primary circuit now into years and built a three-way switch into the circuit so that I could more easily control the polarity and therefore the direction of time travel.

So now I had perfected a time machine by which I could safely sent fruit and mice forward or back into time and then return them to the present. My notes would make an interesting but highly impractical scientific paper. To achieve any useful success, I would have to scale up my apparatus to be able to carry a human instead of a mouse.

I made the assumption that the strength of the lasers and primary voltage circuits would naturally remain constant but the carbonised lead sheet and the electrodes which stood on either side would have to be increased in size. Naturally, I would have to have a larger Faraday Cage built which would take a human subject. Here I planned a slight innovation with the metal mesh cage having an internal insulated floor, a comfortable chair to take a seated person and a simple swing door with a simple latch.

The carbonised lead sheet was no major problem for Mr. McConachie's talents, but the request for a larger Faraday Cage received an even higher raised eyebrow than usual. I gave the Scot a fanciful tale about the need for a bigger cage to test greater three-dimensional ionization effects and hoped that he believed that I was not up to some other obscene activity.

I had already decided that I would be the only subject possible for such a daring experiment as sending a human back into time. Going forward in time did not appeal to me. Apart from meeting myself within my own laboratory, I did want to know what the future held for me and my secure world within the university grounds. Going back in time could also cause some problems for it may cause my Faraday Cage and its bemused occupant to suddenly appear in some room or space which was formally used for another purpose other than my laboratory. I could try this for the first short-time experiment and I would be setting the primary voltage so that I would appear in my own room at a time when I was usually not there; during the term vacation when the room was empty and my apparatus had not yet been set up.

The other problem was how would I be able to control my return if I and my Faraday Cage would be at some other time from the main controls of the apparatus. As this was a matter of time displacement rather than distance, I fashioned a small radio-controlled handset with which I could control the three-way polarity switch, the primary voltage control and the main switch. I tested this unit for over one hundred times and it worked without failure. For these experiments I used a large pumpkin with excellent results.

Finally, the evening came when I would give my apparatus its first test using a human subject; me. I chose a time when I would have been previously at breakfast, climbed into the Faraday Cage and closed its door. I took a deep breath, brought my dark goggles down over my eyes and pressed the main switch on the hand unit. There was the flash of light and an intense feeling of vertigo. Suddenly I was back in my laboratory just as though nothing had happened. I looked across at my old alarm clock and saw that the time was 7:30; college breakfast time. Success so far!

I left the cage just long enough to walk across the room and look out across the quadrangle at the clock tower of St Mary's which was just finishing chiming the half hour. I was slightly alarmed to notice that the hand which opened the window had a faint blue glow surrounding it. I hoped that, as with Herbert, there would be no lasting effects. I returned to my seat, closed the door and readjusted my goggles and the polarity on the handset controls and activated the main switch. A blue flash and I was back in my laboratory with the darkness of evening once again filling the room. Complete success!

I did no more experimentation that evening but strolled down to 'The Eagle' for a celebratory pint. Of course, I dared not tell anyone of the reasons for my happy spirit but just sat smugly in the company of some of the other post-graduate students who were loudly complaining about their lack of success or the over-bearing nature of their supervisors who expected higher standards of research from them.

The thought occurred to me that as and where it stood, my apparatus would have limitations in the time in which to travel. I could be like the character in H. G. Well's novel go so far into the future that buildings would be sparse and well separated. If I went forward in time, this part of the world would still be built over and if the university was still standing, I could end up in some cluttered room or even partway through a wall. If I went back in time, I would have to exceed at least seven hundred years to get out of the university itself and that was not appealing. No, I would have to transport my entire and bulky apparatus to some place where I could rely on any non-interference with urban life.

Making my apparatus portable was not too difficult. It would be bulky for sure, but I reasoned that it would fit within a small box trailer. Of course, the laser mounting would have to have a firm base and my power supply for the primary circuit could be operated from several lead-acid batteries which would be heavy. I would need some help.

It was by chance that Fitzy once more breezed in with his usual 'what ho' and I sat him down and explained my entire experiment and its success.

"Go on!" he said with some incredulity." A Time Machine? You're having me on!"

I reminded him of his pineapple and then explained how Herbert had been transported back and forth with little adverse effects. When I suggested that he try it, he jumped up in alarm.

"Me? All of you scientists are crazy. Why would I do such a stupid thing as to get into your confounded contraption?"

"Alright then." I said with conviction. "Tomorrow is Sunday and the college will have its usual High Tea, right?"

"Year! So what?" his language had become distinctly non-Wodehouse again by now and filled with a little alarm at what I might next suggest.

"Now the Dean as usual will randomly select a passage from the Bible to read to the masses as is the usual custom. If I go now to Sunday evening and find out what he reads and then return with this information and you hear it again when we attend tomorrow, would that convince you?"

"If you could transport the Dean to sometime else, that would be convincing."

"No such luck. He is a man of a previous time to be sure but I doubt that even the founders of the university would tolerate him. So! Is my proof of a successful experiment acceptable?"

"If you can do that then I might start to believe you. Go ahead, I'll stand well clear."

"Good!" I replied and gave him the spare pair of protective goggles. "Sit down and for God's sake, don't touch anything."

I quickly calculated the setting for six o'clock the next night when High Tea would begin and readjusted the dial for the primary voltage accordingly. I climbed into the Faraday Cage, adjusted my goggles and with a cheerful smile threw the switch on the handset.

I had a sudden vision of Fitzy jump with the blue flash from my apparatus and then suddenly he was gone; or more correctly I had progressed further in time. I went back to my room but did not put on my academic robe as was the usual dress for High Tea. Instead, I chose a rather shabby old coat and despite it being summer, wrapped an old scarf around my neck and lower face and donned an even scruffier cloth cap.

I arrived at the Refectory just as the academic staff had progressed in and had taken their seats on the High Table running across the room on its raised dais. I quietly edged my way through the door and stood in one of the darkened corners under the mezzanine above. It was of some interest that I noticed Fitzy and myself sitting on the second table along with the other Senior Students. Fitzy looked up suddenly in my direction and I pulled the cloth cap down over my face. He turned back as the Dean stood up and moved to the side lectern and opened the Bible. He always chose random passages as he had this medieval view that God would direct his hand onto an appropriate reading for the time. He announced that the night's reading would come from the book of James, Chapter 4, Verses 13-15. Noting this down in my small notebook, I turned and left the room and returned to my laboratory.

With another blue flash, I had returned to the startled Fitzy who was still sitting bolt upright in the chair. I gave him the Bible reading and took him to the door where I wished him a good morning and the promise to see him again at High Tea the next evening.

The time for High Tea came and Fitzy and I in our academic gowns took our seats at the second table for Senior Students. The staff processed or rather ambled in as before and I directed Fitzy's gaze to the rather scruffy individual standing well back at the end of the hall under the mezzanine. He gave the figure a brief look and then turned again to the dais as the Dean approached the lectern.

"Tonight's reading comes from the book of James, Chapter 4, Verses 13-15" he said in his high-pitched monotone. Fitzy looked at me with his mouth gaping wide.

"Gosh! You did go forward in time!" he said with even more credulity.

Once the Grace had been said and everyone started eating, I explained how he could help me. I would need the use of his battered old Landrover and his personal help in setting up the apparatus and guarding it whilst I was away in another time. My plan was to drive down to Plymouth near to my home and set up the equipment in a place affording some shelter yet was a time-constant structure which would have been standing for at least two hundred years.

My relaxation away from the equations and figures of physics had been reading about the 'Days of Fighting Sail', that period during the Revolutionary and Napoleonic wars when Britain ruled the waves. This period of time had long been an interest of Fitzy and formed the basis for his current but also long-term studies for his Doctorate into the life of the everyday sailor of the period. I suggested to him that for my own curiosity and for his research, I would go back exactly two hundred years to 1796. Then I could spend a short time observing the nature of old Plymouth and some of the habits, dress and language of local sailor folk. I would try to solve some of his difficult research questions by my direct observations and if possible, would return with some documents or small artefacts of the period.

After High Tea, we returned to his study to consult the many old maps which he had of British naval ports and located an old map of Plymouth dated 1765. Even by that time, Plymouth had developed into a sizeable and well-guarded port and placing my apparatus on a site unencumbered by buildings would be difficult.

By chance, I looked further out from the city and saw the name Mount Edgcumbe. I had remembered it from my childhood. My father had taken us all out for a picnic across the water by the Cremyll ferry and we had spent the day in the area including a walk down to the old folly on top of Mount Edgcumbe. Further research showed that this folly had been built around 1747 to replace an old navigation obelisk but had quickly fell into ruin. The map showed that it still existed today and still in a badly ruined state. There was a car ferry across the River Tamar at Torpoint and then a long roundabout road to Mount Edgcumbe. Fitzy's old map also showed a small track through the forest right up to the folly. This would be ideal as it would be an easy walk down to the village of Cremyll back in time and a good chance of finding a boatman to carry me over the water to Plymouth just as the ferry does today.

With the basics for our plan established, it only meant that the small but difficult details had to be overcome. Transporting my apparatus and its power supply would be no problem but I had now to solve the problem of a twentieth-century man fitting into the eighteenth-century. Friends in the university dramatic society helped me out with my new attire as a travelling scholar looking at the customs of the people of the port city. A plain white blouse with lace cuffs and collar, lace neckerchief, black knee-length breeches with white stockings, black buckled shoes, a sombre grey waistcoat, a long frock coat and a small tricorn hat soon transformed me into someone who should blende into old Plymouth. I had given my friends the excuse that I was going to a fancy-dress party 'somewhere up north' for the weekend.

The main problem was finance. I haunted many of the old antique shops in the town looking for coins which would be appropriate for the time of my trip. The pre-decimal coinage of 1796 would have consisted of farthings, two to make a halfpenny with two halfpennies making a penny. Twelve pennies made a shilling and five of these made a crown and twenty-one, a guinea. We reasoned that a boatman or ferry across from Cremyll would cost at least three pence and some ale at a tavern would probably cost about a halfpenny per tankard. I had suggested that I would buy a cheap notebook and pencil to make my notes so that back in our future time, such a book would then show its appropriate age and give it some authenticity. This book I would then give to Fitzy to aid his own research. A few shillings should be enough for a very quick visit of a few hours but at today's antique coin prices, this amount cost me most of my research grant and some of Fitzy's monthly allowance. I was beginning to think that a modern man going back to the eighteenth-century had more difficulties than I first imagined.

Fitzy had no trouble in taking some time off from his research and so we loaded my apparatus, including the Faraday Cage which had been dismantled, into the back of his old Landrover and set off on a Wednesday morning for Plymouth. We had chosen the mid-week in the hope that there would be few day-trippers and other people around our destination of the folly on Mount Edgcumbe.

Our trip across the English countryside was uneventful and the traffic relatively free on the open highway and so we made good time. We had decided that after such a long journey that we should stay the night in Plymouth and start out early the next morning as soon as the car ferry across the Tamar was in operation. This would get us to the folly when it was probably least deserted. We found a good room in cheap hotel not far from Sutton boat harbour which suited our student income and went for a street reconnaissance after lunch.

Chapter Three

Days of Fighting Sail

It took several weeks and an enormous amount of time for me to acquire a small amount of coinage of low denominations and my dress items for my journey back into the eighteenth-century. During that time, I had some tutoring from Fitzy on the customs and language of the time and also reread some of my own books on the famous captains and sailors of the day hoping to make my senses more attuned for the observations Fitzy wanted me to make. I also made a few slight modifications to my apparatus.

Knowing now that we would probably begin my journey from inside or near the deserted and lonely folly at Mount Edgcumbe, I rebuilt the Faraday Cage so that I could easily detach all of its sides into six panels for ease of concealment with appropriate clamps and latches to rebuild it quickly. I also replaced the chair with a small stool which would now sit on a small square of wood on the inside base of the cage. This too would allow for better concealment.

Fitzy and I spent several nights peering over maps of Plymouth, both old and modern and confirmed that the folly would be an ideal place for my experiment in time. It was in a lonely locality on top of Mount Edgcumbe and whilst the place was now open to tours of the public, it was an extensive private estate back in the eighteenth-century. I planned for us to drive to the folly, if possible and set up my apparatus inside the base of the main tower. Fitzy would guard this whilst I was away and he suggested that he make up, or most likely 'borrow' a sign common to worksites under repair. He would pose as a workman doing maintenance on the old folly and so dissuade any visitors from entering. Of course, I would readjust my return time so that from Fitzy's perspective, I would only be gone for a few minutes even if I should need to spend the whole day in eighteenth-century Plymouth. From my perspective, back in time, I should only need most of a day to wander through the town and glean as much information on the ways of the sailors and other folk which inhabited the dock areas. It would only be the Faraday Cage and its contents which would arrive back in time and I could easily disassemble the cage and hide it in and around the folly. I would have to take the chance that anyone from the Mount Edgcumbe House estate would also not decide to visit the folly on that day.

It was a long way from the university north of London down to Plymouth in Devon, so Fitzy and I decided to leave early in the morning. It took almost five hours to travel the distance but we soon found our accommodation in Plymouth and parked the Landrover nearby. After a simple lunch, Fitzy and I ventured out into the local streets. Our inn was in Vauxhall Street, not far from the boat harbour. We decided to head east down that pleasant street lined with buildings of mostly two or three stories; some modern and others not so but which now still afforded a cheerful aspect. We passed one of the older buildings which had a small, dark wooden shopfront and a sign above the windows reading:

'William Smith & Sons, Stationers
Est. 1792'

I made a mental note that this would be the ideal place to buy my notebook in which I would jot down all of the details which Fitzy would like for his research. A small diary perhaps which would, after two hundred years aging would add to its authenticity when I returned to 1996.

The street turned northwards with several small lanes running off on either side. We turned up one small street which a sign posted on the white, three-storey building of Georgian appearance on the corner read 'Looe Street', it appeared to lead on down to the waterfront. Indeed, across on the other side of the street, another small sign on a post announced that this was the way to Sutton Harbour Marina.

I was feeling excited about being in the dock area of this famous port city, but if I were expecting rows of tall ships with their forest of tall masts and yardarms, I was sorely disappointed. Instead, across a broad, paved carpark filled with a variety of modern vehicles stood but a small and scattered plantation of thin spars now crowded together in a lake filled with the fibre glass and timber hulls of many pleasure yachts. To add to my depression, most of this small, man-made lake was surrounded by modern high-rise units. Drake and all of his later brethren would probably also have stand and wonder what had happened to this cradle of the sea.

Not feeling any joy, Fitzy and I silently turned and retraced our steps back along the bitumen of Looe Street. We continued across the main road, which a sign announced was also B3240 as well as Vauxhall Street, and found that Looe Street now became more in keeping with my faded view of old Plymouth Town. The street was paved with small, neatly lain bricks and the buildings on either side were of an older era, being usually of two stories with fronts of various periods of architecture. The whole appearance was a pleasant one except for the incongruent double yellow lines and parking signs along the sides of the narrow footpaths.

The street was worth exploring, and, as it seemed to head back towards the centre of the city, Fitzy and I continued our morning walk. The street went slightly uphill and continued to be a joy of older buildings with a few small trees planted along one side. Not far along the footpath, Fitzy pointed at a sign hanging from a building further up the street.

"Look Old Fruit! There's an ancient looking inn. That might be useful to our adventure!" he said with some enthusiasm.

As we approached the building, I saw that it was truly an old inn. 'Minerva Inn' the hanging sign and the name over the door announced. It had only a small front, but the white-painted building went up four floors to a gabled roof. The front of the inn was no more than a few paces wide, consisting of two small doors separated by a multi-paned glass window bearing a stained glass figure, supposedly of the head of the Roman goddess of war, Minerva.

I vaguely remembered that my father had once mentioned that the Minerva Inn was one of the oldest in the country and probably dated back to the days before the Spanish Armada. It was closed now but I thought that this would be a good starting place for my research back in the eighteenth-century. I looked at Fitzy and grinned.

"Looks like a good place for some sailor man research" I said. "Nice and handy to the old docks and I'm sure would serve a good ale to assist my observations of its clientele."

Fitzy returned my grin with a 'thumbs up' of approval and so we continued our walk. Our pretty little street soon degenerated at its end into a mass of modern roads and rather ordinary blocky modern buildings, noisy traffic, bitumen roads and construction work. We quickly dashed across a large roundabout through indifferent traffic and continued west along one side of a large dual-laned road which we found on our modern street map to be the 'Royal Parade'. It was not unpleasant, but far from my view of ancient Plymouth. The buildings were for the most part multi-storey and there were several wide, tree-lined malls which added to the cheerfulness of this modern city. We could have been in any one of a multitude of British cities with their bitumen roads, buildings of a variety of ages, styles and colours and, of course, a never-ending stream of cars and lorries.

It was getting late in the afternoon, by now Fitzy and I had walked what we considered to be the length of the main part of the city. Down near the end of Union Street we found an old pub that looked like it might provide some old-world charm, a good lunch and a pint or two. The sign handing over the door read 'The Sailor's Arms' which seemed a good omen and a fitting place to end our hard day's exploration. Fitzy sat down and I went up to the bar where a disinterested bar-tender stood, head down, polishing glasses.

"Good afternoon." I said cheerfully. "Can I have two pints of lager, please?"

The bar-tender looked up with even more indifference on his face and replied in a laconic Australian drawl.

"We only serve Fosters here mate, that'll do?" he said, referring to a well-known Australian brew popular in this country and served icy cold.

"Yes, thank you." I replied. "May I have a lunch menu, please?"

My disinterested bar-tender slapped a single sheet of paper on the bar. There were but a few items listed on the so-called lunch items that my school-boy French enabled me to note that Fitzy was not going

to get his cherished 'bangers and mash'. I ordered two serves of Boeuf Bourguignonne which seemed to be the best on the menu and sat down.
"Well, hardly a traditional sailor's pub!" I said with some exasperation. Fitzy looked at me quizzically. "I doubt that any sailors would frequent this place unless they had just breezed in from the colonies." I continued handing him his cold beer which was well-received despite its not being our usual brown lager.

Our lunch was tasty but certainly over pretentious with its French name. Perhaps a 'tough beef stew' would have been a more appropriate name. Still, it was tasty enough and came with some stale bread rolls which were not. We quickly finished our lunch, deciding not to have a second round of beer, before heading off back along the city streets to our accommodation.

Very early next morning, just as the sun was rising, Fitzy and I went downstairs leaving the key to our room on the main desk. We had paid for our accommodation the previous day and had also purchased some supplies for breakfast and lunch. In a large shopping bag, Fitzy carried some cartons of milk, bread rolls, a selection of cheeses and some oranges. Not exactly two square meals but adequate for the short time which we would apparently spend in the district.

We had planned for only a short but fruitful excursion back in time. From Fitzy's point of time, I would only be gone for a few minutes and we would be back on the road to the university by mid-morning. From my perspective however, I had planned to spend most of the day in eighteenth-century Plymouth but would set my return time so that only a few minutes of the twentieth-century would have passed.

We were lucky to catch the first car ferry across the River Tamar at Torpoint from where it was but a short journey down the A374 to the small village of Antony. Here we turned off onto the road that would eventually wind back along the coast before turning north towards the village of Cremyll and the nearby folly at Mount Edgcumbe.

It was a fine morning so we made good time to the folly high up on the hill overlooking Drake's Island across Plymouth Sound and city beyond. Fitzy had ignored the 'No Cars Please – Coaches only' sign on the side road which bypassed Mount Edgcumbe House and soon we were on the grassy verge next to the crumbling ruin.

It took longer than I had expected to unload the Landrover and assemble my apparatus in the folly. The only flat piece of ground within the folly was in its upper floor by way of a small but narrow stairway. Luckily the space was adequate and cleared of debris. The batteries to power the primary circuit were the heaviest items whilst the stand which held the lasers had to be pushed hard against one wall.

Soon we had the equipment assembled with the Faraday Cage taking up most of the space. I quickly changed out of my modern clothing and donned the garb of my persona, the eighteenth-century student from the university gathering information on the seafaring life; essentially what I had intended in doing in reality. I took the handset with some bread and cheese, from which I had taken their modern wrappings, and stuffed them into one of the big pockets of my frock coat. I checked that my supply of coins was well secured in a small bag in my waistcoat pocket before climbing into the Faraday Cage and placed my small footstool upon the square of wood which was on the floor and pulled my goggles down over my eyes. I was ready.

I had made the necessary calculations and adjustments so that I would arrive in 1796 Plymouth exactly at this day and hour and now was ready for my journey back in time.

"Stand back" I yelled to Fitzy who had already retreated onto the grass outside of the folly. "And don't touch anything. I'll be back in only a few minutes."

"Right you are, Old Fruit. I'll stand guard right here." I heard Fitzy from outside. Then I threw the main switch on the handset. I doubt that any locals across the water would have noticed the bright blue flash which came from their well-known folly.

Suddenly, the interior of the folly reappeared through the glare of the usual blue flash although I noticed that the strange blue glow still persisted over my body. I knew that in a few minutes, it too would dissipate. I looked around and then opened the

Faraday Cage and stepped out into the folly. Thankfully, there were no obstructions in the folly and nobody in sight. The surroundings were as I had left them in the twentieth-century except that the rest of my apparatus, the Landrover and Fitzy were not there. Only the Faraday Cage and its cargo would have been projected back in time.

I quickly dismantled the Faraday Cage and hid the panels in the lower section of the folly. Standing upright in one corner, they looked like simple construction material. The wooden base and the stool were placed high up on a small ledge out of sight and I placed my precious handset into a small, cleft in the crumbling wall under the folly's staircase. A few loose stones and gravel covered the cleft and I was now simply a young eighteenth-century student going for a walk down the hill and through the park to the small village of Cremyll a little over a kilometre around the headland.

Chapter Four

The Girl with the Hazel Eyes

The day was a little different from the one which I had left in my own time. Here and now, the weather was overcast with a cold wind blowing from the south across the sound. There was a small path below the folly which followed the coastline of the headland, known as the Rame Peninsula, around to the village of Cremyll about a kilometre away. I picked up a small branch from the forest on the edge of the path and fashioned it into a walking stick so that I could assume the guise of a well-to-do young man going for an early morning walk. I passed a few people on my way and practiced my eighteenth-century manners by doffing my hat.

Suddenly I heard a commotion further up the path; the screams of a young woman. I rushed forward and around a bend I saw two women being attacked by a small flock of gulls. I had my stick in hand and rushed down the path to their aid, whooping and yelling as I ran. The gulls scattered as I came up to the two harrowed women.

"Thank you, kind sir." The eldest of the two said in a low voice. "They were after the fish which we were carrying in our basket."

The younger woman, who would probably be several years younger than I, looked up and smiled. I was rather taken aback as she was the most beautiful young girl whom I had ever seen. Small and delicate in features with a lovely, open countenance; her shiny blonde hair tied behind her head and hazel eyes which seemed to sparkle when she smiled.

I was lost totally for words for some time and could only admit to being smitten by this young woman. Eventually I came to my senses and stammered;

"I…I .. erh, my name is Tom Sinclair. I am glad that I could help you both," I said, regretting instantly that in my disguise I should have given another name.

The eldest of the two gave the slightest of smiles on what was rather a stern face:

"I am Lady Beatrice Abernathy and this is my sister Lady Abigail. We are second cousins to the Earl of Mount Edgcumbe and have just come down from Edgcumbe House yonder. Our people are up in Sussex so we are here on a short stay. It was most opportune that you should be able to assist us, kind sir."

"Thank you, your Ladyship." I replied, only now remembering my eighteenth-century manners and removing my hat with a slight bow and bended knee. "I am going to the ferry at Cremyll. May I be permitted to escort you at least in that direction?"

"Thank you again sir, for we too are going to that very same ferry, we would be most thankful for your company as I fear that those nasty birds may wish to come back and inspect our fish." There was a delightful laugh from the young Abigail.

"I would be delighted, your Ladyships. Please permit me to escort you both." I replied with some joy.

"As you so desire, young sir." Abigail said with a little laugh.

It was a delightful turn of phrase; one which was uncommon in my age and I delighted in hearing it. 'As you desire, young sir' kept being repeated in my head as we walked along the path.

"And are you from around here Master Tom?" Abigail said with a smile.

"Alas no, your Ladyship. I have just come down from the university to make some notes on the life of sailors in Plymouth town." I responded, not knowing what excuse I could give for being in the right place at the wrong time.

"Oh, well that is most fortuitous" she laughed and put her small, pale arm around mine much to the displeasure of her elder sister. "Our uncle is the Admiral Superintendent over there in The Royal William Victualling Yards, I am sure that he would be glad to be of some help to you." She said pointing with her other arm across the water towards the mass of impressive stone buildings on the opposite headland. "There will be a carriage waiting for us when we land, if you would continue to be so kind and escort us there?"

By now I had completely lost track of my purpose here in time and had fallen into my eighteenth-century character, somewhat smitten by the beautiful girl with the sparkling hazel eyes. "It would be my pleasure, ladies." I said, again removing my hat and making another bow. Arm-in-arm with the beautiful Abigail and with her protective sister trailing closely behind, we continued our walk along the path to Cremyll. The sun had suddenly emerged from the clouds to match my mood, I was a happy man.

Cremyll was a small but neat village of single or two-storey cottages and a rather respectable-looking inn, the Edgcumbe Arms with cream plastered walls and a steep grey shingle roof. I was reminded from my recent research in the area that this region was considered part of Devon in the eighteenth-century and that the road through Cremyll and its small ferry was then one of the main routes into Plymouth from the west.

We walked down to the end of the main street to a small rectangular stone building with a flat roof which stood on the water's edge. It had a window where one could purchase tickets for the ferry. Beyond this was a grass-covered stone wharf at the end of which was the ferry. This was unlike any ferry which I had used in my own time. It was essentially a long rowing boat with a long, rigid ramp at its front to take on passengers and cargo and a flat area at its centre reaching back to the stern. This area could accommodate a horse or two and perhaps a small cart. Six men were grouped around the end of the wharf near the ferry; some smoking, others enjoying an early breakfast.

I took out my small bag of coins with which to purchase tickets for the three of us. The notice near the window stated that each person should pay tuppence with three pence for a horse and six pence for a small cart. I was trying to do a mental calculation as to my financial state and this new unexpected expense when Abigail lightly touched my hand and whispered into my ear:

"Oh no, dear Tom. The ferry is owned by our cousin at the House and you must be our guest. That is the least we can do for our bird protector." She laughed in her sweet little way.

 We walked along the wharf to where the ferry was tied up beside which a group of men were sitting on some stone bollards:

"When does the ferry leave, Henry?" Beatrice asked the eldest of the group of men who suddenly stood up and removed the pipe from his mouth.

He was obviously the captain of this distinguished vessel and he brought his knuckle up to his weather-beaten brow and said with a broad smile he said:

"Why yur Ladyship, when e'er ye fancy an; we'l be orf."

She thanked him for his courtesy and climbed on board, moving down to near the stern where she adjusted her voluminous skirts and sat down on one of the wide seats which ran across the width of the boat. I helped Abigail into the boat where we joined her sister at the stern.

"Nah then, lads! Let's be orf an' not keep the ladies and the young gen'leman a'waitin'" Henry the boatman said, turning to his mates and throwing the single mooring line on board. He moved past me to the steering oar at the stern whilst his companions took up the five large rowing oars near the front of the craft.

With a deft movement, the crew turned the boat around and headed out into the expanse of water which separated the Rame Peninsula from the opposite shore. I judged that this was only about three hundred metres away but already the wind was beginning to whip the water up into small wavelets.

I realised then that most of the naval vessels in Plymouth occupied anchorages off to my left, that is up into the estuary River Tamar which Abigail called the 'Hamoaze'. Fitzy and I had been incorrect in assuming that the main anchorage would be within the city itself. In the Hamoaze there were anchored ships of the line, a couple of sleek-looking frigates and some smaller vessels. All had their yards secured with sails neatly lashed to them. This seemed to be the main base of the Royal Navy as it still is today. Still, I had resolved to explore the eastern part of Plymouth where Fitzy and I had been the previous day. Time permitting and with some considerable regret, I would spend only a short time with Abigail, her sister and uncle. Afterwards I might explore some of the taverns nearest the naval base before walking back to my original targeted research area.

The sun had broken briefly through the clouds and the waves in the Hamoaze had flattened somewhat allowing them to sparkle in the morning sunlight. Things were looking up. Our little ferry did not land on the adjacent headland as I had supposed it would, but went past on the western side of the headlands.

"Them's be the victuallin' yards o' the navy, young zur", Henry the steersman said pointing to the long rows of stone buildings on the point which we were now passing. "Not tha' the food is any god, ya mind beggin' yur pardon yur Ladyships!" he continued with a snort and steered the ferry over to a long stone wharf on our right, just beyond the naval yards.

"Here we be!" he said with a little pride "Safe und sahnd at the Admiral's Hard, yur Ladyships "

The vessel touched the side of the wharf with a gentle bump allowing one of the forward oarsmen to jump ashore to secure the vessel to a stone bollard.

"This be Stonehouse here und Plymouth proper is abarht aft a mile ta tha East." The steersman continued for my benefit. "Ye'll find Edgcumb Street and then Union Street jus' up tha road ta take ye inta tarnh. Gud day ta ye yur Ladyships an' ta ye too, young zur."

I thanked the steersman and his crew and put some of my precious coins into his hand as I stepped ashore. There was a small, closed carriage standing nearby, black in colour and with a small coat of arms emblazoned on its door. The driver jumped down to open the door with a slight bow.

"Welcome your Ladyships. Your uncle is waiting at his rooms." He said with the low voice that servants affect when performing their duties and gave me a quick, dark look.

"Thank you, James." Beatrice said to the driver and she and Abigail climbed in and I followed with the door being shut quickly behind me. The carriage started up along the cobbled road which ran back along the waterfront. Rounding a small curve, I saw a rather impressive stone arch coming up. The red-coated marine on duty stood to attention and brought his arm across his musket in salute as we passed.

The carriage rounded another corner and stopped outside an impressive large, two-storey stone house with another marine sentry standing at the top of a small flight of stairs. He saluted as we walked up the stairs and into the vestibule of the building. Gazing around me I had noticed that the building stood on the edge of a large, grassed park surrounded by similar grey stone buildings all edged with small bushes with pink flowers.

A portly, bewigged man in a blue frock coat covered in gold braid, brass buttons and medals came down a wide oaken staircase to greet us.

"Why, Beatrice and Abigail! What a pleasure to see you both again. Welcome to my humble quarters.

And who is your gallant escort?" he said turning towards me with a quizzical smile.

I decided that it may be of some embarrassment to allow Beatrice to explain that we had only met that morning and that I was simply their protector from seagulls, so I again made my low bow and introduced myself.

"Doctor Thomas Sinclair, your Lordship." I said with some formality.

"Ah! You're a Physician, then?" the Admiral exclaimed.

"Alas no, sir. Just a humble academic down from the university to make some humble observations about the lives of the simple sailor," hoping that my quest would not seem an invasion into his territory. The old admiral gave a slight bow:

"I am Sir Grenville Gascoyne, the Admiral of Royal William, and your statement is most gratifying, young man. There has been considerable discontent amongst the jack tars, especially concerning their low pay and conditions. I and some of my friends, especially Dickie Howe, have been concerned about their plight for some time and have been pressing the dolts at the Admiralty to rein in some of their flogging captains and give the men some greater care."

I sympathised with the admiral, as he seemed to have a good heart and genuinely cared for his sailors. I knew also that in the very next year of 1797, the mutinies at Spithead and at the Noire would soon shake the complacency of the Royal Navy.

The admiral called his servant to order some tea which was very well received by the ladies and myself. For my part, I had not taken much to eat since early that morning in the twentieth-century. Our conversation ranged from small-talk about conditions at the time, I was particularly interested in the admiral's views on conditions at sea and the need for better food and equipment; a topic in which he himself had a professional interest. His comments would be very useful for Fitzy's research, especially considering the events of the current time which would lead up to the future mutinies.

Eventually, time passed much too quickly and the admiral stood up from the table and apologised for the need to take the ladies to their quarters and for him to get back to his business of supplying the Royal Navy. I also apologised for my need to get on with my research in Plymouth town but I was sorely reluctant to leave the beautiful Abigail.

"Forgive me ladies, but I must regretfully take my leave from such pleasant surroundings and your good selves, for I too must get on with my observations." I said, trying hard to hide my lie and disappointment.

"As you desire, young sir," said Abigail, "but we will miss your company, won't we Beatrice? We are going back on the ferry tomorrow morning. Perhaps we could meet again, Doctor Thomas Sinclair." She said, turning to her sister who gave a noncommittal nod of her head.

James, the coachman suddenly appeared and Sir Grenville put me into his care to drive me over to the centre of Plymouth town. I thanked the admiral and gave a last goodbye to the ladies; my eye making a meaningful contact with the sparkling hazel eyes of the lovely Abigail.

It was difficult parting from her, but I turned and followed James down to the waiting coach which would take me into Plymouth. The coach turned into Edgcumbe Street and then into Union Street towards my proposed locale of research. Previously, Fitzy and I had estimated that it would be about a two kilometre walk from the western edge of Plymouth, that suburb derived from the town of Stonehouse, and my target area near what was then called Sutton Pool where we had first encountered the modern yacht harbour.

I was saddened to leave Abigail and even more so that we would never meet again, but somehow, I felt strangely at home in this bustle of eighteenth-century life. There were no cars nor lorries; nor were there the great crowds of people scurrying in a hurry to get to nowhere in particular. I had to watch where I was going to be sure, as there was still a reasonable crowd of people in the street. Their pace was much slower than back in my time and it was nice to get a warm greeting occasionally from some passer-by, especially a warm smile from a 'comely lass' with her basket of vegetables as she walked home from the nearby market.

Union Street was still a major thoroughfare of Plymouth town with horsemen and the occasional cart or carriage which would pose a problem as I walked down the street. I would quickly jump aside, and soon learned to look where I was stepping after a short slip on a pile of horse manure, one of many in the paved street. There were no footpaths as yet and I noticed that some of the smaller side streets were unpaved. Still, the air was fresh, apart from the earthen smell of the horse manure and some open drains of sewerage in some side lane.

Naturally there had been much change in the buildings and the streets from this time to my own, but I eventually found Vauxhall Street by random wandering from some of the older buildings which I had remembered and its proximity to the waterfront. A little way along it I found my stationery shop. It still had that old casement window but now it was freshly painted and the sign above the door simply read:

'William Smith – Stationer.'

I pushed open the little door and went in to the jangle of a small brass bell attached to one of its corners. I was greeted by a youngish man dressed in similar garb to my own except that his hat and frock coat had been removed and that his waistcoat was a sombre brown.

"Good morning to you sir, how can I be of assistance to you?" he said in a well-educated voice.

"Would you have a small pocket diary – nothing expensive?" I enquired.

"Certainly, sir. I have just the ticket!" he said, walking to the rear of the small shop which was full of rows of books, ledgers, bundles of paper of different colours and neat glass-fronted drawers of pens, pencils and ink bottles. Opening one small drawer, he brought out several small, well-bound diaries. He gave me the range of prices which varied from a few pence to several shillings for one bound in Moroccan leather. I chose one of the smaller and less pretentious books which cost me sixpence. I paid him the price out of my dwindling supply of coins in their small bag and thanked him for his courtesy.

I left the shop with some smug pride for I now had a useful diary in which I could jot down all of my future observations in this interesting time. I was also pleased that when I opened my little book, I found a small pencil held in a loop of cloth at the back of it. Success indeed. I felt a little like a schoolboy who was on excursion in a foreign land and had successfully purchased an object of his desire without too much difficulty.

It was just a short walk along Vauxhall Street and then a sharp turn into Looe Street to my next destination, the Minerva Inn. I was pleased to notice that little had change in Looe Street, except that some of the modern buildings had yet to replace some of the stone cottages and that there were more trees and no cars on its sides. There was, however, a steady stream of people walking down both sides of the paved street and a few vendors pushing hand carts.

The Minerva Inn also seemed to have defied the changes of time. The paint was still black but a lot more faded than the refurnished one by which Fitzy and I had passed two hundred years in the future. Looe Street was now just one of the older streets in the town which had considerable use. It had yet to be 'rediscovered' by a future generation seeking to revitalise the past.

I went in where I was met with a pleasant air of stuffy conviviality. It was darker than I imagined and quite small for my concept of a sailor's inn. The wood panelling was brown and old, probably dating back to Drake's day, but now also highly polished. For this time of mid-morning, the inn seemed crowded and the clientele actively engaged in loud conversation with the occasional coarse words, laughter and yells:

"Anutha pot o' ya best, Moll if ya please!"

"Garn, don tell me tha' the old *Bellona* was faster than the *Athena*! Neva!"

"Hey, Jockjo! Cum an' sit wif us, mate!"

"Oy, landlord! Were's tha scran ye wuz promisin'"

My entrance was not regarded with much attention, even if my dress seemed somewhat more formal and cleaner than most. It was obvious that most of the patrons of The Minerva were seafarers from their faded white canvas trousers, small pea jackets, neckerchiefs, cloth or tarred hats and a variety of other items of apparel that one usually saw in old painting of the times. I pushed through the crowd who were standing around the small bar near the middle of the room and found an opening at a table in the far corner. The men at the table were friendly enough and pushed along to let me sit down.

"'ullo, matey! An' where'r ye from? Ye don' look like a tar ta me." Said my nearest companion with an amiable smile.

"No, sir. I've just come down from London. I'm an apprentice there in a bookbinder's stores. I brought some rare books down to one of the stores hereabouts." I lied as I thought that an intellectual from the university come to study the sailors of this town would not be received as kindly as a simple bookbinder's apprentice on an important errand. I had chosen that occupation on the spur of the moment; my hero of science, Michael Faraday having been just such an apprentice and had educated himself in science by reading the copies of the Encyclopaedia Britannica which he bound.

"Wot's yur name then, matey?" my new companion
asked.

I thought that my title and even my name would be
a little out of place in this inn of boisterous eighteen-
century sailors, so I answered.

"Tom Jenkins sir, an' I'm please to meet you an' your
mates."

"Well, nah, matey, yor've wif a bunch o' the finest
tars in al o' Britain ere! So, don't ye worry. I'm Jem
and this 'ere thin pole nexta me is Will." He said in
a friendly tone. He then stood up and yelled across
the room. "Ay, Moll! Brun us a pint o' ya best ale fa
this yun gentlmun, will ya?"

It did not take long before a buxom young barmaid
came over with a foaming tankard of ale in her hand.

"That's a farthing, Jem, an keep yo voice dahl'n. Id'll
wake even Davy Jones imself!"

I brought out a few coins and found a small farthing
and offered it to Moll the barmaid but Jem gently

push it aside and handed her one of his coins instead.

"Nah, matey. Yo're a noo 'and ere, and we uve just bin paid off, like so ave plenty o' loot."

"Thank'ee, Jem." I replied, now feeling confident with eighteenth-century language. Jem and his mates had just come off an East Indiaman ship from a very successful cruise to the Indies and were feeling mighty happy with the world.

"Ya!" said Willy leaning around Jem. "Wiv jus' got back see, an we dun alrigh wif our traden. An we 'av our Protecshuns from tha' Press so we are free o tha sea fo a mite." He said happily, bringing a piece of parchment out of the inside pocket of his jacket.

"Put it awa' Will, ya idjit! Tha's too many tars ere tha wud nick tha orf ya, smart like!" Jem sternly said and pushed Will's arm down out of site.

Chapter Five

Pressed!

The strong ale and the gregarious nature of the company was going to my head. My attempts at making notes about the clientele of The Minerva would have to wait until later and then done from memory.

Jem and his mates had, like most sailors newly ashore, had been most generous with their money and were happy to share their bounty with a humble bookbinder's apprentice who was new to the town and had just stopped in for some company and perhaps one pint.

When I expressed my thanks for their generosity, Jem explained in a quiet voice, quickly looking around the room as though he was divulging a state secret and then looking at his mates for conformation, that they indeed had 'plenty o' loot' from their 'little ventures'. It was the custom of sailors of the Honourable East India Company to do their own private trading in such things as rich, embroided silks, spices and other eastern luxuries for sale when they reached England. Whether the Honourable East India Company officially condoned such trading was never discussed, but it seemed to be a common practice amongst the sailors. Such 'extra benefits' of eastern deployment of ships and the purchase of popular items at local wholesale prices was probably still going on in my own time.

Willy, the obvious clown of the group was boldly showing me his latest tattoo, a newly acquired custom of tars sailing to the east and to the Pacific. Suddenly the front door of the Minerva burst open and a rat-faced looking man burst into the crowded inn, a look of abject horror on his pock-marked face.

"Watchit mates! The Press is cumin' duhn tha' street!"

The crowded inn erupted in noisy panic as men looked around them for a way out to evade the dreaded Press Gang which was about to invade their carousing.

"The press!" Jem said with some natural alarm and then sighed and sat back, relaxed in his seat.

"It allis right, mates! We 'ave our Protecions wif us, aint we?" he said with a satisfied look.

Protections were the documents issued to sailors and other necessary occupations which exempted the bearers from naval service. These were especially granted to merchant seamen, especially those employed by the postal and revenue services, men of the fishing fleet and those of powerful trading companies such as the Honourable East India Company.

Jem suddenly looked around at me with some concern:

"Look matey, them's be afta prime seamen like, but a 'ealthy young genlemum like yo'self would alsa be a catch. Yu'd betta skidaddle, Tom"

I caught his meaning and looked around for a way out. There was only the front door which was now crowded with a group of men struggling to get through it. They suddenly all fell back in a disorganised heap as several burly sailors in tarred hats and blue pea jackets burst in. All were well-armed with evil-looking cudgels.

The rat-faced man who had raised the alarm had pushed through the crowd to a far corner of the inn where he stood and yelled over the frantic screams and shouts of the panicking sailors.

"Dahn 'ere, mates!" he yelled in his high-pitched voice as he lifted up a large trapdoor in the floor of the inn. It obviously led down into the cellar where the inn's beer kegs were stored. He jumped down the first few stairs and was hastily followed by a group of scared men. Being nearby, I gave Jem and his mates a quick look of appreciation and followed.

It was dark down in the cellar, save for a small light some distance along weakly coming through the mass of heads of jostling men. Others behind me pushed frantically to gain the security of the cellar before being caught by the Press Gang behind.

Ratface had gone well ahead of the crowd of escapers and had pushed up and open two large cellar doors which opened out onto the rear courtyard of the inn. He stood at the base of the steps and exhorted the men to hurry:

"Quick-like, nah lads! Up an' ouht afore the Press git ya!"

We stumbled and half fell out of the wide mouth of the cellar door – right into the waiting arms of a circle of rough-looking tars, some holding evil-looking cudgels and others holding coils of rope.

"Welcome to tha Andrew, gents!" one of them said as we fell about on the cobbles of the courtyard. Some of my colleges tried to make a run for it; some succeeded and managed to scurry over the wall of the courtyard. Others like myself were grabbed by some calloused hands.

"Hold on, tha, matey. I got yer nah! Or do I 'ave ta let me sweet Betsy giv' ya a kiss on yer 'ead afore ya go ta sleep." With that, the weather-beaten and ugly tar who had grabbed me tightly on the shoulder waved an even uglier cudgel in my face.

I was truly scared. Here was something that Fitzy and I had not considered in our plan to observe eighteen-century sailor life. I fell to my knees in genuine horror but managed to have the wit of survival to keep in character:

"Oh please, sir. Don't press me. I'm just a poor apprentice come down from London on an errand. I'm no sailor." I begged.

I was unceremoniously jerked up to my feet by the powerful grip of the seaman.

"Them's the way of the wurl, me lad. We'll soon make ya a jolly tar. Don' ya worry abaht that." He said with a smirk whilst tying my hands with a short length of rope.

He half led me and half dragged me over to another group of men who had already been caught. Another member of the Press was tying them onto a long length of rope forming a tight chain of captives, not unlike old lithographs I had seen of convicts or slaves being led to their destinies. Another captive, an old sailor with a faded jacket and an untidy long grey beard, looked me up and down and then spat onto the cobbles.

"The Andrew mus' ave bin getting, mighty desparat' takin tha likes o'yo und me" he said with some despair looking venomously at the Press Gang now finally 'processing' their personal catches. It was then that I noticed the rat faced little man standing to one side in the corner of the yard, his hand held out to an untidy looking officer who was now counting some coins into his hand. We had been caught by a professional.

The untidy looking officer completed his business with ratface and sauntered over to his new line of captives. His uniform was generally grubby and not well made. It had the white tabs of a Midshipman on its collar although the man himself looked to be well past his prime.

"Right lads! Let's get this scum back aboard. There'll be a good tot fer all of you when we get 'em back." He said with some false familiarity.

There was a sudden jerk of the main rope and we were pulled along out of the gates of the inn's courtyard and into the street. It was late afternoon, and the cry of 'the Press' had ensured that most on the street had quickly found shelter indoors.

Occasionally, there would be some cry of derision from an anonymous window above, but in the most part there were only the sobs and cries of the pressed men; mine amongst them. This was the accepted way of things in this difficult time of war.

We had emerged into a narrow lane which ran back into Looe Street, a little way down the street from the inn. Our forlorn procession noisily made its way across Vauxhall Street then on towards the boat harbour of Sutton Pool. I had trodden these streets once as a free man, now I was one of His Majesty's pressed men.

Our little group of captives arrived at the stone pier on the western side of the Pool where several ship's boats had been tied up. We were half pulled and half pushed into the stern of one of the waiting boats. Amidst a gaggle of men in all states of orientation, I felt a lot of netting beneath us in the bottom of the boat. Gradually we were able to find our positions in the hull of the boat and to sit upright.

"Now my lovelies! No nonsense now" said an educated voice from out of the darkness. "You are all now in the King's service, so you will have to make the most of it."

There were more sobs from my companions and pleas for release.

"I av a wife un family a' ome!" cried one.

"Please let me go. I'm jest a poor 'prentis!" said another.

I was too stunned to say anything, so just lay in the bottom of the boat. I was able to free my hands a little and with some difficulty extracted my small, and as yet empty note book out of my coat pocket and pushed it down into the front of my breeches. I hoped that no one would search there. My hat had been left in the inn and somewhere in the mayhem, my small bag of coins had been lifted.

"Giv' way a' tha bow. Giv' way a tha stern" came a cry in the darkness and the mooring ropes were tossed unceremoniously into the boat. There was the wooden 'clunking' sound of oars going into rowlocks and then the boat was pushed off from the stone wall of the wharf.

"Eave ho, me lads! Let's git this nice bag o' fish back ta tha ship. Quick smart!" said the anonymous voice from the stern.

There was nothing more to do. Occasionally, one of our forlorn group would try to stand up and would be roughly pushed back down by a cudgel or oar. I looked over the side of the boat to see the feeble lights of Plymouth town slowly receding into the gloom. It was late afternoon by now, the sun had set below the threatening clouds of a storm.

After some considerable time of rowing, the anonymous voice again; this time with some pride:

"Thar she be!" he called. "His majesty's Ship *Thaleia*. *'Old Thaly'* we's calls 'er. Tha best frigate in tha 'ole o' tha navy."

I turned around and raised myself slightly up to look over the bow, passed the heads and shoulders of the oarsmen. It was indeed a beautiful ship. Low and sleek in the water, painted black with a broad yellow stripe along her entire length. Her gun ports were open, no doubt to let in some fresh air. She had three masts but her sails were still tied up tightly to her cross spars.

"You'em be lucky lads tha we'em be needin' sum more 'ands, tha *Old Thaly* bein' a bit short o' tha momen'. Thar she be! Thirtah-ate guns she 'as. An biggens, too! Eihteen pohnders an' som' o' them new carronades'. Tha poor Frenchies won't know whot hittem!" Came the voice once more.

There was a heavy bump as the crew brought our boat alongside the hull of the *Thaleia*. A stout rope with a hook on its end came down into the boat where several of the crew pushed and shoved our little band as the cargo net below us was attached to the hook. Up we went, like so many fish in the net that was dumped unceremoniously onto the wooden deck.

"Form up over there!" said the educated voice which came from the scruffy Midshipman who had just emerged through the opening in the ship's side. He was now back in his own element and appeared to take some pleasure in exerting his authority.

Our hands had been untied and we shuffled together as an uncoordinated group over to the other side of the deck where the scruffy officer was pointing. Not far from us was a group of red-coated marines standing ready, bayonets fixed to their muskets. Two blue-coated officers watched the proceedings with some apparent boredom from the Quarterdeck above.

Suddenly a forceful stream of cold seawater was played upon us. Some of our number fell over onto the deck and the rest of us tried to shield ourselves from the powerful stream. There was laughter from some of the idle hands and from our Press Gang who were now standing on the deck out of range. All of the so-called 'sanitation process' being completed, a couple of sailors threw us some dry clothing of various descriptions then we were told to form an orderly line. This led to the front of a small desk further along the deck. Seated at this desk was another officer, elderly in appearance who had just opened a large ledger and was dipping a quilled pen into a large, ornate ink bottle.

"Name, place of birth and rating or occupation, if you please, gentlemen." He said in a loud voice with a hint of sarcastic formality.

It was then that I was shocked to see both Jem and Willy, my friends from The Minerva also standing on the deck a few paces in front of me. They had been spared the 'sanitary process' and were still in their best clothes from the day at the inn. Jem caught my eye and I and bleakly looked back and shrugged:

"Sum bugger dropped tha King's Shillin' inta ohr ales an' called us bloody 'voluntairs'! So here we all ar' then! Sorry ta see ya got cought an' all, Tom." He said with genuine pity.

When Jem got to the table he said proudly:

"Jem Jackson, Plymouth, Voluntair AB, sir!"

Willy was quiet and gave his details in a soft voice. Like Jem, he was unhappy to be here, but he was not proud to admit it. When it came to my turn, I was lost for words but stammered:

"I shouldn't be here, sir. I'm not a sailor. I'm an apprentice from London, sent down to Plymouth on an errand." I heard myself saying in a quivering voice. The elderly officer looked up without any show of emotion on his face and asked bluntly: "Name?"

I told him my name was 'Tom Jenkins' and then looked down to his ledger and wrote as he spoke:

"Tom Jenkins, London. Landman. Next!"

I was pulled away from one of the hands waiting nearby and another officer, a Petty Officer by his dress and bearing, spun me around and pointed to an opening in the deck.

"Gun Number Four, larboard. Get for'ard an' find the mess wif an foor' onit. Get!" he roughly shoved me so that I half fell along the deck and into the gloom of the raised forward deck.

Chapter Six

Shipmates

"Bless me nah! Who's this 'ere wet pollywog?"

The good-natured enquiry came from a big, full-bearded man sitting at a wooden table which had been lowered down to rest upon one of the eighteen-powder guns. Several other men sat around the table.

"Is this gun Number Four, larboard?" I asked, the cold of the early evening beginning to get to my bones.

"Right ye be, matey! ye 'ave come to the best gun mess in tha ship!" with that he stood up, having to bend over slightly so that his head did not hit the timbers above. "Pressed man, huh? Well, nah, git outa them wet things and sit yo'sel down. Hey Taffy, rig a line o'er the gunport for this here noo shipmate." He said talking to a small, dark-faced man sitting near the open gun port. "An' Paddy, thro' a blanket frum tha' bin to this wet squab." He said to another big sailor next to him.

I took out my small diary which thankfully had escaped most of the hosing down and put it onto the bare table. Stripping off my clothes in somewhat of a self-conscious manner, I folded the proffered blanket around my wet shoulders and sat down on the end of long bench which ran the length of the table.

Paddy reached up to a small alcove near where the roof met the hull and produced a large, black bottle. He grabbed a metal cup from a row of cups on hooks and poured some brown liquid from the bottle:

"'Ere nigh. 'av a drop av dis' in yer." He said in a lilting Irish brogue." Dohwn in wan swollow nigh!"

I took the cup and swallowed and then gasped for breath. Neat rum! It went down like fire but it certainly took the chill out of my body. There was some gentle laughter around the table at my discomfort.

"Well now, matey! Ye ain't a sailor, that ther's the truth in it. What was ye before the Press invited ye to sign on, lad?" said the big man with the black beard.

I coughed again and said in gasps of air:

"I was a bookbinder's apprentice. Come down from London with some books. I was pressed before I could return."

"An a'prentiss was ye? well, I'm Bob Clarke so's everyone calls me 'Nobby' like all the other Clarkes in the navy. Wot's yer name then, mate?"

"Tom Jenkins" I replied, giving them my new, assumed name.

"So's ye cann readden an' writenn cann yerren Tom?" said a sandy-haired young man from the other side of the table. His accent came from one of the Scandinavian countries.

"Yes, a little." I lied. It would not be a good idea to flaunt my university education amongst these men. I was beginning to learn that a Doctorate in Nuclear

Physics would not be much use around here. Nor for that matter, most of the rest of my education. Learning had changed over the two hundred years which separated these men and those of my generation. I would have to rely on my early primary schooling and perhaps my interest and reading about the 'days of fighting sail'.

"Ya, dat be most usefool as ve losts our only scholaren overboard in der lass' sturm ve 'ad. Ve cood do viff some'un who cann reader der lettrs vhich our luve ones senden to us," said the fair-haired man.

"Aye, dat's roit!" said Paddy. "We lost pur 'arry o'er de side in'a storm in de Bay o' Bisky only las' week. kip be 'is soul. Tha's why we ar' in port, ter refit loike."

Nobby moved around to the end of the table and looked down its length with a smile.

"So nah fer some quick introdoocions. You've herd frum Taffy Evans und Paddy O'Hanlon an' that tha blonde yung'un, as ye can guess is Swede Larson, our' powda monkee what's gets the charges frum belo'. Finally, thar's Scrounger Smith at the end o' the table, the best sea lawya and fixit man on tha ship'. "

Each man in turn gave some sort of acknowledgement as his name was called and I tried my best to return the compliment. They seemed to be a good bunch of fellows and it was obvious that Nobby, who was the Gun Captain of Number Four larboard gun, was a good leader.

The introductions over, the men got back to their activities whilst Nobby took me aside and explained the setup. The ship was divided into several distinct groups according to its function at different times. For general organisation and discipline, we were broken down into small Divisions, each under a junior officer and for the purposes of the safety of the ship, there were two watches, Larboard Watch, and Starboard Watch. Lastly as far as occupations were concerned, we were gunners whose main function was to handle the ship's armament. On board the frigate *Thaleia* of 38 guns, we manned one of the 28 larger 18-pounders but there were also eight nine-pounders on the Quarter Deck above and two six-pounder guns on the foc'sle. Whilst rated as a 38-gun Fifth Rate Frigate, the *Thaleia* also carried six additional guns on the Quarterdeck and four on the foc'sle. These additional weapons were 18-pounder carbonnades or 'smashers' as the crew preferred to call them. They were short, stubby, smooth-bore guns of wide calibre produced by the Carron company at Falkirk, Scotland and mounted on slides. They could fire an eighteen-pound ball or devastating canister shot of many smaller balls over a short range. They were infamous for their destructive power at close range.

As we were a larboard gun, that is on what is left-hand-side of a ship facing forward, we were also in the Larboard Watch and rostered in keeping watch over the ship on a generally four-hour period. The exception to this was during Action Stations, drills or when changing sails. During the first two events, our station was at Number Four larboard gun which its crew had affectionately called 'Thundering Tilly' after one of Nobby's loud and foul-mouthed aunts.

At any time, the hands could be expected to be called upon to handle the ship, including the gunners. We were expected to handle the 'sheets' which were ropes attached to the sails or the 'hal'yards' which moved the yardarms or cross booms which held the sails. All of these actions were to be done by us and the rest of the deck crew whilst the 'topmen' went aloft and handled the sails from above. These were considered to be the elite members of the crew, even better than gunners, but only just so according to Knobby. During Action Stations or a drill for this, others of the crew not involved with the guns would take our places as 'deck handlers'.

There were other members of the crew including the 'Idlers'; a term which I found fascinating because in my modern time, this term implied anyone who did little work and generally wasted time. Here however, they were simply another section of the crew; those who's important occupations meant that they did not have to stand watch. The idlers included people such as the Cook, Sailmaker, Purser and their assistants as well as the Steward's mates and various servants to the Officers.

The Officers also varied in their ranks and functions. Above the crew were the Petty Officers including the Quartermaster in charge of watch-keeping, the stores and steering the ship, the Boatswain or 'Swain' who generally looked after the functions of the ship itself and the Midshipmen who were trainee Officers.

Above this group were the Warrant Officers, so called because they held 'warrants' promoting them to this rank. They too had a diverse range of functions aboard the ship. They include the Sea Officers such as the Master, a very important officer who was generally in charge of operating and navigating the ship and the Purser or 'pusser' who looked after the purchasing of stores and the ship's finances. A much-maligned figure, the pusser could be most efficient or most corrupt depending upon the vigilance of the Captain. The ship's Surgeon was also considered a high-ranking Warrant Officer. Other Warrant Officers who were considered inferior to their sea counterparts included such as the Cook, Armourer, Surgeon's mates and on some ships, if obtainable, were the Schoolmaster and Chaplain. Depending upon the Captain, some frigates discouraged the latter two functionaries.

Above all of these ranks were the Deck Officers. These consisted of the Lieutenants, the number of which varied according to the size of the ship. The *Thaleia* carried a Third, Second and First Lieutenant, the latter being the Captain's second-in-command and the person who mostly saw to the overall naval operation of the ship. 'Jimmy-the-One' as he was often called by the crew behind his back, or simply the 'Number One' could be a hard task master as required. Usually, they were promising officers who were promoted through merit but some could still use brutal methods in maintaining the discipline of the ship through a set of cronies in the lower officer ranks. Lastly, there was the Captain. He had the overall responsibility of the ship and its tactical use as dictated by his Admiral. Most captains were competent, good tacticians and cared for their ship and crews, but others had bad reputations as 'floggers' who used the lash or 'cat-o-nine-tails' as the only means of controlling their crew. By 1797, the abuse by some of these officers in the Royal Navy and the corruption in all the subsidiary supply chains and depots precipitated several mutinies amongst ship's crews at Spithead and at the Noire. In these matters, the *Thaleia* was a lucky ship, having a generally good set of officers and a happy crew.

Dry and feeling warm again from the change of clothes, thanks to the generous sea chest of the lost seaman Harry and the rum, I opened my little diary and wrote down the pretentious title 'A Diary of Tom Jenkins, Pressed Man'. I had tried to recall all of my adventures ashore, especially my impressions of Old Plymouth town, its streets and people and especially the clientele and boisterous good bonhomie of The Minerva Inn. My heart fell somewhat when I recalled my meeting with Abigail and her sister and I had much sympathy with poor Jem and Will who were tricked into 'volunteering' for this very ship. I wrote down everything which Nobby had told me about the workings of the ship and of the people who manned her and my particular place in its function. I was just noting down the latter when there was a hushed cry from Paddy:

"Watch ooeht now mates! 'ere combs Mr FitzAdam."

I was struck by both the sudden interruption to my writing and the name of 'FitzAdam'. I quickly closed my diary and slid it under the table, resting it on the barrel of the big gun beneath it.

Mr FitzAdam was our Divisional Officer, a young Midshipman who would be no older than perhaps sixteen years of age. His blue uniform coat was well-

cut and relatively plain except for its single row of
brass buttons and the white tabs at his collar. He
held his cocked hat under his arm as he walked up
to our table. Nobby stood up and knuckled his
forehead in salute.

"Gud evenin', Master FitzAdam. an' 'ow would ye
be keeping?"

"Fine, thank you Clarke" he said with a smile on his
youthful face. He seemed a well-presented young
man and from the reception of my new shipmates
was respected amongst this crew. I later learnt from
Knobby that he was an earnest young man,
intelligent and not over-bearing, considering that he
was in fact the Right-Honourable Alistair FitzAdam,
the son of landed gentry somewhere in Sussex. I
could not but help to wonder whether or not he was
some ancestor of my friend Algernon FitzAdam
who also hailed from that county.

My thoughts went back in time, or rather forward to
the twentieth-century and I thought of my friend
Fitzy standing guard over my apparatus inside the
folly at Mount Edgcumbe. It really would not matter
how long I spent in the eighteenth-century provided

that I had the opportunity to return, but I would have to readjust the settings on my handset controls to get back to just a few minutes after leaving my friend two hundred years in the future.

The young Midshipman turned slightly and looked down at me, still sitting with my mouth open at the end of the table.

"Ah, you must be Jenkins, I take it?" he said with a smile. "Welcome to the *Thaleia*. I see that you have been lucky enough to join the best Division in the ship. What?" He said with a little laugh.

Nobby grinned and looked around at his mates who all nodded with approval at this complement.

"Beggin' yo pardin, Mr FitzAdam zur, but this 'ere noo recroot is a Landsman, like." Scrounger spoke up from the end of the table, taking advantage of the good nature of the situation. "'E should't be a pressed like 'e wus, zur. Wif all doo respect."

"Thank you, Smith." The young officer said with a look of pained concern on his youthful face. Turning to me he said:

"Do you have any proof of your status, Jenkins? According to the law, you should not have been pressed, but unfortunately that is but a small consideration in these desperate times."

I gathered up my wits and replied:

"I am sorry, sir, but I was a bookbinder's apprentice travelling down from London and have no proof at all. All of my papers and belongings have been taken from me." I lied, not wishing to divulge my true status as a nuclear physicist from two hundred years in the future.

"Well then, I'm truly sorry, Jenkins. I will put your case to the First as the Captain is still ashore, but I doubt that you will hear any more on this subject. All I can say is that you accept your fate and feel lucky that you are on a good ship such as the *Thaleia* and not a flogging ship like as many as I could name."

I gave the Midshipman a weak smile and knuckled my forward. "Thankee, sir. I will try to do my best in the line of duty."

What else could I say. I had no chance of immediately getting ashore and back to the folly and to my own time. I would have to wait until such a time presented itself. In the meantime, I would have to play my role as the pressed landsman and do the best I could. At least I had found 'a comfortable berth' as my shipmates referred to their condition, and the young Midshipman seemed a good officer.

"Oh, by the way Jenkins, the Officer-of-the-Watch wants all new men on deck right now if you please." The young Midshipman said as he turned to continue his rounds.

That statement, whilst given in terms of good manners was an order needed to be carried out immediately.

"Thankee, sir." I said again stood up, knuckled my forehead and turned towards the open deck.

It was beginning to get dark as the sun was starting to set over the distant town and the low ground beyond. I came out onto the main deck with some caution and joined the forlorn-looking group of men standing in front of the main mast. Two officers strode up with a confident air:

"Right! I am Mr. Jamison the Third Officer and this is Mr. Midshipman Harris" the tallest of the two men said. With some uncertainty, I noticed that the other officer in a grubbier uniform was the same elderly Midshipman who had presided over the Press Gang which had raided The Minerva.

"Carry on, Mr. Harris," the Third said as he turned and quickly left.

"Al' right, you scabby swabs! "said the Midshipman, "We're looking for some new Topmen, see. So, we're goin' to have an 'up-and-over' to find out what you're made off."

He pointed up the mainmast to its first landing or 'top' at the first part of the mainmast and said:

"Up you's go and across the top and down t'other side. There's the ratlin's over there so up you go!" with that, he hit the closest man on the buttocks with a short length of knotted rope.

Jem and Willy literally knew the ropes and quickly jumped up on to the side of the ship called the gunwale, or usually the gun'le, and then onto the ladder-like rigging that came over it from the outside. The 'ratlines' were the thin cords of small-diameter rope which stretched across four stout wire-ropes which formed the 'standing rigging' which went up to the first top and helped secure the mast.

Jem and Willy were both experienced hands at such an action and quickly clambered up the rigging and reached the top of this lower section of the mast. These came backward from the stem of the mast to the outside edge of the broad platform of the top and were known with some dread as the 'futtock shrouds'. Here, the climber would have to hang backwards and virtually climb from underneath the top with their feet and hands defying gravity.

Jem and Will simply went around the front edge of the top, bypassing futtock shrouds and moved quickly across the platform of the top and began climbing down the other side. Most of the other men in the group had similarly climbed up the rigging and were now just reaching the top. I had little choice and so I also climbed up onto the gun'le and began to climb. I had remembered the advice during my early student days of rock-climbing in the Lakes District where my old instructor had said 'always three points of contact – two hands and a foot, or two feet and a hand'.

Up I went. One rung or ratline at a time. I noted to my horror that some of these thin, tar-covered cords had been broken in places; a repair job for some reluctant sailor given extra duties.

I had no difficulties climbing up to the top, and whilst I was totally scared doing it, there was some little pride in achieving such a task. Arriving at the top, I found that hanging upside down or stretching right over a long drop to go around the side of the top was going to be difficult. It was then that I noticed that there was a small, but negotiable hole cut into the top between its outer edge and the mast. This was the 'lubber's hole', a safer way onto the top for inexperienced 'lubbers' like myself. I went through it, across the top and down through its counterpart on the other side.

I arrived back on deck as the last man, much to the grins of the experienced hands but I felt a little elated that I had achieved such a task.

"Well dun', matey" said Jem in a whisper. I was beginning to feel a part of this ship at last.

"Right! You and you!" the old Midshipman said, roughly grabbing both Jem and Willy by the shoulders in turn. "You're now Topmen see, on the foremast, upper topsail. Now all of you other swabs get back to your billets."

I walked back to Number Four gun and proudly told my friends of my climb to the first top.

"Betta 'ere on deck!" said Scrounger. "Too many ar' wanta fall orf in bad weava, see?" He said with dark humour.

Nobby had lit a lantern above the table and we all sat down. The ships bell had just wrung at eight bells at the end of the First Dog Watch. Swede Larson had explained to me in the broken English that the hours onboard ship was regulated by the chiming of the shops bell. This also denoted the start and end of each watch. They were every four hours with the bell being chimed by the current Quartermaster's Assistant every half hour which was in turn determined by the turn of the half-hour sand glass; the duty of the lowest Officer-of-the-Watch.

The only exception was the two Dog Watches; the First starting at four in the afternoon and the Second starting two hours later at six. These were inserted into the watch times so that the roster of the watch bill would not cause any watch to be on at the same time each day. Bells were rung every half hour as with the other watches except that there were eight bells rung at the end of both Dog Watches to tell the crew that there was a change in watch keepers. The term 'Dog Watch' was a fascinating expression to me which had an unknown derivation. Some said that as the first of the night watches, it was a time when everyone, including dogs should be asleep. Others maintained that it referred to the first sight of Sirius, the 'dog star' in the early evening sky.

In general terms, Nobby explained that the main watches were the First Watch which started at eight bells and at eight o'clock, the Middle Watch which started at midnight and was not liked by sailors, the

Morning Watch at four in the morning, the Forenoon Watch at eight in the morning and the Afternoon Watch starting at twelve. The bell was rung at one bell after the first half hour of each watch and increased in number every half hour until the last eight bells at the end of each watch. There were only two Watches teams onboard the *Thaleia*, Starboard and Larboard, which meant that, apart from the Dog Watches, members of each watch would do watch-keeping for four hours and then four hours off for sleep. Not that this occurred regularly, as there was always something to do during daylight hours.

Now at eight bells, the end of the First Dog Watch, Nobby looked around our mess table and said:

"Oose the Mess Cooks for tonight?" Taffy and Paddy grinned and stood up. "Nah, don' fogit ta tell Cook tha' we av' a noo 'and. Right! Giv' im a wink und a nudge frahm me, see – an' he owes me some slush for them favas I did 'im. Tell 'im!"

It was the duty now for two of each mess to take the wooden pails down from their hooks on the deck head, or ceiling, and go down to the galley or kitchen where the cook would fill them with the food which was allocated for that evening. Today being a Tuesday, we would be having 'salt junk' as the main ingredient. This was salted beef which probably would have been in the keg for years and now boiled down in the Cook's huge stove in the galley. The 'slush' which Nobby referred to was the yellow grease which floated to the surface when the meat was boiled. Cook, or 'Slushy' as he was often called, would sell it to the crew so that they could smear it onto their biscuits. This latter food item came in the form of very hard round or square thrice-baked bread which was often stale well before it reached the ship. Moreover, it was common to find maggots inhabiting these biscuits. These were removed, at least in part by banging the 'hard tack' biscuits on the table and any which still remained considered as extra fare. Some wise old hands helping in the galley might catch some fish and lay them on the bags of biscuits to entice the maggots to migrate up to the fish. Often as not, these 'bargemen' who 'sailed' the biscuits on the sailor's table would simply be tolerated and eaten.

Apart from this daily ration of biscuits, bread if in port such as tonight, the sailors were each given eight pints of beer – about four and a half litres. The idea was that water on board ship was often not fit to drink, although there was a 'scuttlebutt' of water, a half keg; kept on the deck for regular sips. More to the liking of the sailors was the 'grog' ration, served twice a day in the mid-morning and mid-afternoon. This consisted of a pint of strong navy rum watered down with a quart of water, that is about one-and-a-half of diluted rum. The term 'grog' is said to have come from about 1740 from the nickname of "Old Grog" for Admiral Vernon because of the cloak he habitually wore made of a coarse kind of taffeta called Grogram. He unpopularly introduced the watering-down of the sailors' rum in the hope that this would reduce much of the drunkenness onboard navy ships. It failed!

Sailors have a way of circumventing any such official actions aimed at curtailing their few pleasures. A wink and a nod to a friendly Quartermaster's Assistant and some 'neaters' or raw rum might find itself into the sailor's tankard. It was also common for sailors to store this raw spirit, as in the black bottle hidden up near the deckhead in our mess, and occasionally share it with messmates. On Number Four gun mess, this was considered to be a cooperative venture as all of the crew were considered good-mannered 'sippers' not 'gulpers' who swallowed large amounts nor 'sandy-bottoms' who drank it all. Drunkenness was still rife aboard ships and it was a flogging offence to be found drunk on duty. Off duty was another matter.

After a while, our 'mess cooks' arrived with the cooked beef, bag of biscuit, a small barrel of beer and a large tin mug full of greasy 'slush'.

"Gud oh!' said the Swede who began to distribute the plates, spoons and tin mugs from their secured shelves and hooks in the bulkhead. Each of us sat around the table whilst the two cooks stood at its end with the table with the pail of beef stew. It was the custom in each mess for the cooks to turn their backs on their mess mates and dish up the stew first before asking who should receive it.

A plate was filled with stew and one of the mess cooks, with their back to their messmates would ask: "Who's to receive this plate." A name was given and the plate was then handed along to the named sailor. My name was the first called and the plate passed along had a generous portion of the over-cooked beef. The small keg of beer, the pail of biscuits and the tin of slush were placed into the centre of the table.

"Well, nah! The cap'in as dun us proud. We 'av some vegables in ahr stoo!" Exclaimed Scrounger, pulling out some chunks of turnips and carrots from his plate. This was generally thought of as being something extra and so then the salty concoction was called 'lobscouse' and was usually only available whilst in port. At sea, the rations would be sparer and of the traditional stale kind.

The meal progressed with some animation of discussion, along with the occasional banging of the bread on the table. This act was more of a habit than a necessity as the bread had only recently come from the Royal William Victualling Yards on shore. Whilst bitter, the beer was a welcome draft to the saltiness of the beef and the rancid taste of 'slushed' biscuit.

Some of the men from a nearby mess came over to join us, bringing their own tankards of beer. I was introduced and was able to successfully convince my new shipmates that I really was just a poor apprentice from London newly caught up in the local Press. There was the usual sympathy about my introduction to 'the Andrew' but a general feeling of comradery, considering that most of these men, experienced sailors now, had been press at one time or another.

I was just getting to enjoy my new life in this mess when I heard eight bells ring from the end of the Second Dog Watch. Eight o'clock. There was a sudden, high pitched trill of a pipe. It consisted of two short blasts followed by along high-pitched trill which dropped for a couple of seconds and then went up to finish on a high note.

"Pipe Dahn, mates." Said Nobby and our quests quickly left whilst my shipmates put the plates, mugs and cups into the pails to be washed early the next morning. The table having been cleared, it was lifted up on its hinges forming a secure cover over the shelves of spare plates and cups. Next, my shipmates went over to the centre of the ship and pulled out long rolls of canvas, bound by several well-spaced loops from wooden bins. Each man untied these rolls to reveal canvas hammocks which they then secured to hooks set in the deckhead. Nobby showed me how to untie a roll and the hooks where I should 'sling my hammock'. Having set them up as a neat row so that they hung parallel to the side of the ship, each man in turn used the various beams in the deckhead to leap up into their hammock. Nobby showed me how to do this so I was soon comfortable under a blanket and swaying like my fellows with the gentle swing of the ship. Nobby blew out the candle in our lantern as the deck settled down to night routine. It had been a long and very eventful day for me.

Chapter Seven

In All Respects Ready....

Ding-ding, ding-ding – four bells in the Morning Watch with the grey light of dawn just beginning to creep through the open gunport. Six o'clock in the morning and I rolled over in my hammock as it swayed gently with the roll of the ship. I had been awake for some time thinking about my future, here back in the past. I had found that the persona of Dr. Thomas Sinclair, Bachelor of Science with first class honours and Doctor of Philosophy, nuclear physicist, had little use in this world. Tom Jenkins apprentice, on the other hand had found a foothold here with some good friends but a very doubtful future.

I recalled from my leisure reading of history about the Days of fighting Sail that the *Thaleia* was one of the most famous frigates of its day. It had been well-commanded and manned and had fought many a famous action, sometimes with heavy losses but its crew had always remained faithful even through the infamous mutinies of the next year.

There was nothing more for me to do but to continue playing my new role and taking down all of the details of life on board the ship until such time that I could return to Plymouth. It therefore become a matter of routine for me to write in my little diary all of the trivia and fine details of frigate life which the history books overlooked. My new shipmates from my mess would take this as an eccentricity of a man with some education. In this role I could also be of service to them as it was on some rare occasions that they would receive letters from home, probably dictated by their loved ones to a Parish clerk or the Vicar himself. In return, I would take down their dictation for a word to go home at some later date.

There came a sudden long trill followed by several short blasts of the Bos'n's call:

"Rise and shine, show a leg, show a leg!" came the call of the Master-at-arms who walked briskly down the lower deck waking up those unfortunates who had probably been on a late-night watch. The 'show-a-leg' call referred to the times, still common, when sailors would have their 'wives' on board and so they would have to throw a feminine leg over the edge of the hammock so as not to be disturbed.

My watch had been on the Middle Watch which had finished at four in the morning, so I barely had time to unlash my hammock and jump into it. Like the rest of my mess, I swung down onto the deck giving myself a good shake. Scrounger had been as resourceful as ever in raising a pail of seawater up through the gunport for those who wanted to wake themselves up. Washing was not a great priority, as freshwater was scarce and sailors preferred to keep their 'natural body oils' undiluted. Once used, the excess would be thrown overboard. These pails would be then used for washing the utensils and dishes from the previous night, also in seawater with some waste holystone for an abrasive.

There was much to do as we soon found out. Petty Officer Jarvis came along the larboard messes with a big grin on his face and several pails of sundry items.

"Nah then, gennelmen, we 'ave some polishin' ta do." He said as he handed out rags, pails of fresh water and several jars of neatsfoot oil. This was a yellow oil which was used to condition and to help preserve the timber of the ship which often sustains much use, especially the ship's railing along the top of the gun'le. We would work in teams with the first member wiping the rail with a rag dampened in freshwater, then came the next who would dry it with another rag, and finally the 'oiler' who would give a generous coating of the oil to the timber. Not a difficult task, but there was a lot of timber to be oiled. The other onerous task was polishing the large amount of brass work on board.

By six bells in the Forenoon Watch we had once again taken up our watch stations. The last of the water hoys, or small tankers used to refill the water barrels of the ship, had just cast off when there was a loud hail from an approaching launch.

"Thaleia!" came the cry. The use of the ship's name meant that this launch carried its captain. There was a minor panic as the junior Officer-of-the-watch, our Mr. FitzAdam, sent runners for the senior officers and the Captain of Marines. The later was Captain Bedford Spotswood, a very dapper officer whose red uniform always appeared to be immaculate regardless of the weather, contrasted with the blue of the other officers.

The Bos'n's call sounded the 'still' with its long, low note going to a long high note and then back down for an equally long low note. At this, all of the 'old hands' who were not employed on deck took cover whilst the rest stood still facing the open entry port where the captain would enter. By now the side party had mustered on the Quarterdeck to receive the captain. This party consisted of two groups: Captain Spotswood and a line of his red coated marines standing at attention; and another line opposed and facing them consisting of the senior deck officers starting with the First Officer, finishing with the Third Officer. Others kept out of the way.

The captain's head appeared over the edge of the entry port as he stepped up to enter the deck of his ship. The officers and Captain Spotswood doffed their hats and the marines brought their weapons to the front of their body in salute. In reply, the captain doffed his hat and shook hands and said a few words with a smile to the First Lieutenant. He then moved directly to the ladder leading to the Quarterdeck with its railing and mesh wall filled with rolled hammocks. He stopped for a moment and looked out over the main gun deck of his ship. The Boson piped the 'Carry on' and then in a loud voice called:

"All 'ands on deck. All 'ands on deck. Muster aft!"

The cry went through the ship and every man who was not actively engaged in handling the ship tumbled up to form a large crowd on the main gun deck below where the captain stood. I had been watching these proceedings with great interest from the shelter below the foredeck, then moved out to join the rest of my shipmates near the back of the attentive crowd.

Captain Edward Trevallyn was a youngish, but never-the-less, imposing man. A little over average height and broad in the chest, he looked every inch the commander of a frigate. He wore the blue coat with twin rows of brass buttons and the epaulettes of a Post-Captain. His face had a friendly, benign appearance and his jet-black hair had already started to turn grey around the temples. Nobby told me that he came from a distinguished Cornish family well-known for their service at sea. He was not a 'flogging' captain Nobby had remarked, but he brooked no nonsense when it came to duty and the running of his ship. He also had the reputation of being a fair-minded man, and I gather from the adoring looks of the men now assembled below him, that he was a popular leader. He stepped forward and placed two large hands onto the railing:

"Well lads! We are back again and in all respects are ready for sea." He paused for a short while and looked around at his crew and gave a small grimace. "I am truly sorry lads, but we are back on blockade again in the Bay of Biscay and there we might have to pick up a Frenchman or two."

This last comment raised a ripple of laughter amongst the men for they had been lucky in the past and they had all benefitted from the prize money which they received. The *Thaleia* was considered a lucky ship. The captain continued:

"You will be all pleased to know that the Dons have decided to join their neighbours and also come out against us. Well, they will just have to take their turn to become one of our prizes."

There was a good deal of laughter at the news that the Spanish had now joined the French against England and that the captain considered this threat as simply more opportunity to take even more prizes. Captain Spotswood standing a little way from the captain simply slapped his thigh and muttered his usual comment:

"Good show! Extra training value."

Very little flustered Captain Spotswood, Nobby confided in me, and this comment about 'extra training value' was often made, especially when things looked desperate or the odds were against them.

Captain Trevallyn stood back from the railing a little and raised his hat:

"Here's to another good cruise, my lads. God bless the King! Now, back to your duties, for we will be setting sail shortly."

"Three chars fa tha' cap'in and good King George!" came an anonymous voice from within the crowd. And the crew responded with three enthusiastic cheers whilst waving their hats.

The twitter of the Bos'n's call came from behind us and the loud voice of the man himself:

"'Ands aloft ta' make sail. 'Ands ta tha capst'n to weigh ancha'"

"That'll be us, matey." Nobby nudged me in the shoulder, for it was our turn on watch now and raising the anchor was part of our deck duty. The capstan was the vertical windlass which was used to raise the anchor or to heave the ship off any sandbar if we were unfortunate enough to run aground. It was a large, round vertical drum with many spokes which took the 'capstan bars' which were inserted into sockets around its sides. We grabbed the bars from their housing nearby, then took our place behind each bar before starting to push the capstan around. From somewhere a lone fiddler appeared and jumped up onto the middle of the capstan. He started up a shanty or seaman's song which was often sung to help the men with their task. There was singing mixed with a grating sound as the anchor cable came up and slithered its way down through the hawse-holes into the cable tier below. The men sung with gusto; one man calling the verse, the others repeating the final words of each line, then singing the chorus:

"Well, I joined her on a cold December morning
(*morning*)
A-flapping of me flippers to keep me warm **(keep me
warm)**
With the south cone hoisted as a warning **(a warning)**
To stand by the coming of a storm

CHORUS
Paddy lay back, (Paddy lay back)
Take in your slack (take in your slack)
Take a turn around your capstan heave a pawl.
'Bout ship, stations, boys, be handy (be handy!)
We're bound for Biskay in the morn.

Well, I woke up in the morning stiff and sore **(sore)**
And I knew that I was outward bound again **(bound
again)**
And a voice come a-bawling at the door **(door)**
Lay aft men, and answer to your name **(to your name)**

CHORUS
Paddy lay back, (Paddy lay back)
Take in your slack (take in your slack)
Take a turn around your capstan heave a pawl.
'Bout ship, stations, boys, be handy (be handy!)
We're bound for Biskay in the morn.

And so the shanty went on with our crew making up verses along the way; usually derogatory ones in jest about their shipmates, the French or the Spanish. There was significant laughter between the verses and soon the anchor chain clattered up the side. Then another team ran to the ship's side to secure the anchor with the fish tackle or ropes attached to the top of the anchor which would attach it to the cathead, the projection which held the anchor away from the wooden sides of the ship.

Above us the sails billowed out in turn from the ends of the yardarms in towards their centres as the topmen, standing precariously and bare-footed on the footropes below the yards, undid the gaskets which had held the sails to the yards. The buntlines and clew lines, ropes attached to the bottom and corners of the square sails respectively were then hauled down by the deck crews who secure them to the belaying pins below the gun'le.

To me this was a magnificent sight; the white canvas sails were like some gigantic wings which were now moving us slowly out of the Hamoaze and into the open waters of the English Channel. To add to the beauty of the scene, the sun came out through a break in the clouds, glistening across the water.

We rounded the Eddystone Light and from the position of the sun on our larboard quarter, I estimated that we were now headed roughly south west so that we would eventually pass the island of Ushant before heading into the Bay of Biscay proper.

The next day the wind was unexpectedly calm as we were still in the protection of the Lizard, that long Cornish peninsula which juts well to the south into the Channel. It was a good time for the captain to exercise the great guns of the *Thaleia*. Now I was to learn the fine points of my new trade; Tom Jenkins – Gunner.

The *Thaleia* had been brought round into the wind, the sails once more hauled up to their yards as we hove to; we were now drifting with the wind and tide. A boat was lowered and barrels, each bearing a pole with a large red flag attached to it, were towed around to each side of the ship to act as targets at about a hundred metres from the ship. The target looked small even at this short range, for Nobby proudly boasted that our gun could fire an eighteen-pound iron ball up to a little over 2500 yards, two kilometres in my time, given a maximum charge and elevation of about ten degrees. In battle, such range was usually not a consideration as ships often battled at close range with their yardarms touching. The range also depended upon the type of shot fired; ball or round shot being the usual shot, but canister and chain shot was used at closer range, especially canister which fired a great swarm of musket balls over the enemy's decks. Chain shot required more finesse as it consisted of a hollow ball, split in two halves which were joined by a length of chain. This would scythe through the air and hopefully cut the rigging of the enemy's ship. Today we were only using round shot.

Nobby and the others had cleared away all of the items after breakfast; these had been washed and replaced into their selves, and our mess table once more hauled up to its vertical position against the interior of the hull. We were now 'all squared away' and ready for action. We were lucky because Captain Trevallyn, unlike most frigate captains, believed in exercising his gun crew to a high degree of speed with accuracy. To do this, he had purchased extra powder and shot out of his own purse.

Our gun crew of six had specific functions with each man being assigned a number. Nobby was the Gun Captain and so he was Number One; aimed the gun, primed the powder and then fired it with a lanyard attached to a flintlock trigger mechanism. Paddy, being a big man was the Number Two who turned and raised the gun barrel using blocks and tackle to swivel the gun around and then knocked in or out the wedge-like quoin below the gun's end to raise or lower its barrel. Scrounger was the Number Three man who loaded the gun with powder, wads and shot. This was a very important job and could be a dangerous task in the heat of battle; it required close attention to the proper sequence of loading. First Scrounger would shove the gunpowder charge down the barrel; this was usually a cartridge bag made of cloth or parchment. After the charge, a wad of old canvas or rope was then rammed home with a pole rammer. Next the shot was rammed in, followed by another wad to prevent the cannonball from rolling out of the barrel if the muzzle was depressed. Taffy Evans was the Number Four man, entrusted with the task of swabbing out the barrel after each shot with a long pole with a wet rope swab at its end. This was to ensure that there were no sparks remaining in the barrel when Scrounger pushed down the gunpowder.

I was given the lighter task of the Number Five man which was to pass the ammunition and help Paddy move the gun. The young boy, Swede Larson was the Number Six man or 'Powder Monkey'. His task was to run down to the ship's magazine secured well below deck and bring back the canvas charges to the gun.

As this was my first lesson in gunnery, Nobby went through all of these tasks in a loud voice as they were being performed for the first time and the rest of the crew used great exaggeration and great good humour as they carried them out in a most theatrical manner. Young Swede Larson arrived with the first bag of powder and scampered up and down like his jungle namesake making guttural sounds waving his arms over his head.

The gun carriage was then 'run out'. Paddy and I heaving on the gun tackles until the front of the gun carriage was hard up against the ship's bulwark with the barrel protruding out of the opened gun port. As part of the drill, I helped Taffy swab out the gun even though it had not been fired for months, then Scrounger loaded the powder bag, swab, heavy ball and the second swab.

Swede moved aside the buckets of water and spare swabs to a safe distance then once more rearranged the pile of spare round shot on their brass holder or 'monkey', a general name for several types of ship's holders or carriers. This usually was only produced on deck and temporarily placed at a safe distance from the gun when it was to be used as loose round shot rolling across the deck was dangerous. I thought with some humour that the weather was not yet cold enough to 'freeze the balls off a brass monkey' but I did have some doubts as to truth of this phrase.

Nobby poked a small metal taper down the touch hole of the gun to break open the charge bag exposing the gunpowder. Next, he rearranged and cocked the flintlock mechanism which would send a spark down to the powder when he pulled its lanyard. He squatted down and peered along the barrel of the gun, motioning with his outstretched hand the direction Paddy and I were to haul on the tackle to aim the gun. Using a rough estimate of distance, he told Paddy to hammer the quoin in a little with a wooden mallet to reset the elevation.

"Numbrrr' For' Gun, ready!" Nobby called, holding his left hand up above his head and his right hand wrapped around the end of the long firing lanyard.

Mr FitzAdam, our Divisional Officer, had been nervously walking up and down the gun deck watching each crew perform their various tasks. During the heat of battle, it would not be uncommon for the swab man to forget his task or even for the loader to leave his ram in the gun. He had to watch everywhere at once; a difficult task for a sixteen-year-old boy. Now, there was neither the panic of action nor the need for speed. This was the first shot of the drill and Number Four was the first gun ready. The second shot and third shot would require more speed and frantic teamwork as the young Midshipman would be timing the rate of loading and firing with his pocket watch.

"In turn, Number One gun leading, shoot!" called Mr FitzAdam in the loudest voice his young lungs could muster.

"Boom, boom, boom" the big guns fired in turn and I could see several small water spouts coming up around the target.

"Stan' clear, mates!" shouted Nobby who pulled his lanyard. 'Thundering Tilly' fired with an enormous noise and a great cloud of black smoke filled our confined space. The noise was deafening even if I did have my hands held tightly over my ears. The acrid smell of gun powder and its soot swirled round our gun position.

"Haul awa'!" Yelled Paddy as we pulled the gun back so that Taffy could swab out the barrel. The gun all loaded again, Nobby yelled:

"Stan' clear! Run ourt!" and Paddy and I once more pulled on the tackle as the barrel went out through the gun port.

"Stan' clear, mates!" shouted Nobby again and once more 'Tilly' thundered. Two more shots were taken and two more patterns of small water spouts straddled the small target. We hauled the gun back each time and Scrounger again swabbed out the barrel. After the third shot, the rest of our crew turned where they stood to look at Mr. FitzAdam who was now marking down some details on his small slate. It was a short time before he looked up and around the gun deck with a grimace on his face.

"Three shots in seven minutes and no hits! Not too good, lads. We're going to have to do better next time." He said and walked off to make his report to the First Officer who was in charge of the gunnery practice.

"Aye, mates!" Tha' not gud an' all," said Nobby disgusted with their performance. "We've shooda dun it in five!"

We 'stood down' our gun and Scrounger threw out the water from our swab tubs through the open gun port, scowling as he did so. We lowered our mess table over the hot gun while Paddy pulled down our black bottle from its hiding place. It was not yet time for the morning grog, but a little boosting of our spirits was sorely needed as we again made sail.

The rest of the day continued on its usual routine, in the evening, Swede lit our little lantern and we got ready for our evening meal. Tonight, it was Pease

Pudding, or at least a variety of pea soup made from dried, split peas and perhaps any ingredient left over from the night before; perhaps even some salt pork. There was the usual ship's biscuit, small beer and navy cheese. This last item was particularly well-known to sailors as being very hard, almost indigestible. It was an insult to that lovely county by calling it 'Suffolk' cheese. Certainly, it kept for some time, but old hands often said that rats, attracted by its strong odour, would gnaw a hole in the barrel to get to the stuff but could not even make a tooth mark in it when they got to it.

We had eaten early as we were on the Second Dog Watch at six when most men had their evening meal. It was only a short, two-hour watch before we had some time for brief relaxation afterwards until 'pipe down'. Up on deck, gazing out over the gently rolling sea with the brief spells of silvery, shimmering moonlight playing across the water, I had time to think about the day's gunnery practice. Here, perhaps was an area where my twentieth-century education might finally be of some use. Previously I had felt despondent that a man of my advanced education was totally useless in this day of sail with all its complexities and customs totally foreign to me.

Now, the ballistics involved for firing a cannon can be quite complicated and involve many variables. However, there were so many rough estimations in the use of the eighteen-pounder which took a matter even basic physics to a questionable level of accuracy. If I were to apply my knowledge, I would have to use what would be available and also consider the people who would be making use of it.

I knew from my early undergraduate days that the maximum range of any gun could be calculated by knowing its muzzle velocity, and the angle at which the gun is fired. In mathematical terms, this came out as:

$$\text{Range} = v^2/g \times \sin 2\theta$$

The value of v, the muzzle velocity of the gun could be taken roughly as a constant, assuming that the charges were fairly uniform and standard. Rather an optimistic view, but I had no other way of ensuring that the charges would give a constant velocity. I could find out the muzzle velocity of our long guns from the Master Gunner who would know such technicalities. The value for g, the acceleration was a constant at 32 feet per second per second and so all I had to do was to find the range and then I could calculate the angle of elevation of the gun.

Of course, I now needed a table of sines to use in the equation. Not having any tables, I would have to construct one myself from the well-known ratios for the angles of 30^0, 45^0 and 60^0, although, as I was told that our gun usually fired at angles around 10^0, the larger angles would not be needed. It was a relatively simple task to calculate a range of sines from 0 degrees (=0) to sine 30^0 (=0.5) with each sine going up about 0.17 per degree. Now all I had to do was to find how to measure the range to our target with more accuracy than the guesswork usually applied.

For this, I remembered my early lessons in parallax and the basic concept of rangefinders which I had also read about. I thought about this, then devised a simple hand-held rangefinder that would be only very rough but again better than simple observation and guesswork. I drew up plans for a simple hand-held T-shaped device with two small tubes resting in the top of the T. One would be fixed at one end and the other pivoted on a point at the other. The observer would look through both tubes as in using a pair of binoculars and then rotate the pivoting tube until the target came into the vision of both eyes. Using trigonometry again, I calculated the angles which would correspond to different ranges as given by the hypotenuse of the triangle thus formed when the target was in view through both tubes. Naturally, all of this would be just so much useless numbers and figures to my shipmates, so I decided to have the range simply given as angles to which the gun must be elevated.

The next problem was how to accurately measure the elevation of the gun? Then I remembered a lithograph which I had seen in an old physics book. This showed an old cannon with a right-angled triangle sticking out of its muzzle. The right angle of the triangle was subtended between the projection from the muzzle and that side hanging down; the hypotenuse was replaced by a curved side which was marked off in angles. A plumb line handing down from the point of the right angle therefore gave the angle of elevation of the gun.

The next day, when not on watch, I approached the Master Gunner, Mr. Johns. I explained to him the device which I had seen and he gave a hearty laugh:

"Why;m lad, Tha' be a Gunner's Clinometer!" he said cheerfully. "I 'av one jest like it below in tha arm'ry".

Encouraged by this, I persuaded him to show me the device so I could then trace its dimensions onto a piece of paper with a pencil. He also gave me that the muzzle velocity of his long eighteens was 1720 feet per second.

I now had all of the information to calculate angles from the range and plans for a device to measure it. I explained what I needed to make this device to Scrounger Smith. I also had devised a way to make a simple gunsight to line up any future target instead of simply looking over the muzzle. After I had explained what I wanted, he gave me a queer sideways look and with no questions asked touched the side of his nose with his index finger and said:

"Leav' it wif me, Guv." And then with a sly look: "But id'le cost yer a sippers?"

I thought that a share in my afternoon grog ration was worth it, so I gave him a wink and a nod and he quickly left. Scrounger was certainly a character. Nothing was impossible for him; nothing was too difficult to procure – sometimes with a price, sometimes not. He also had the unique ability to come and go so quietly that he would suddenly appear or disappear at any given time. I sat down to make some final touches to my calculations.

It took a while, but suddenly Scrounger appeared by the mess table where I was working and dumped a pile of material onto its top, much to the consternation of the rest of the gun crew.

"Sorry mate, but id'le cost yer too sippers, like. I 'ad ta promis' one ta Mr. Buckle, tha' Arm'mra fo' tha metal toobs."

Thankee, Scrounger." I said with a smile. "Well worth it."

I looked around at my shipmates who were now very curious as to what I was up to with the various bits and pieces that now lay on their mess table.

"I'm sorry, Nobby." I said looking up at the curious Gun Captain sitting across from me. "I should have asked you first, but here is a way to ensure that 'Thundering Tilly' hits the target every time."

This aroused significant interest now, and the men moved up along the benches to look at the pile of small pieces of wood, metal sheet, nails and a small hammer. I looked up and smiled at them:

"As a book-binder's apprentice, I also get to read the books that I help bind. I had remembered after our disappointment the other day at gunnery practice that I had read of how some of the artillery pieces in forts were more accurately fired." I lied.

I showed them the outline of my rangefinder and Mr. John's clinometer. I also explained how I would make a more accurate gun sighting device using a vertical nail held by tar mounted on the centre of the muzzle and a vertical metal sheet with a sighting hole in it which would be attached to the end of the flintlock device at the other end. The men looked interested but I could see that it was over their heads. Nobby was the first to speak up.

"Well, nah, Tom. If'n yer think tha' all've this will do tha' trick, then do let's do it. Mr FitzAdam tol' me tha' we've bin 'avin anutha gunnry shoot when tha' wevver is fine. We shood show'em 'ow we shoot then, 'ay?"

There were cheers from the rest of the crew. Looking around at their enthusiastic faces, I set about constructing my devices with a curious audience.

Chapter Eight

An Unexpected Move

"For exercise, for exercise. Hands to quarters, hands to quarters!" came the Bos'n's loud cry followed by the rata-tat-tat of the Marine's drums beating to quarters. It was a fine day; the breeze was gentle and we were seemingly in the middle of nowhere.

Up on the Quarterdeck, the Carpenter and some of his mates were lifting up another large target barrel with its large red flag over the gun'le and into the sea.

Mr. Johns the Master Gunner came striding down the gun deck ducking his head below some of the beams as he was a relatively tall man. He said in his booming voice:

"'Ere we go, lads. Tha' Captain is goin' ta exercise the big guns under sail. We've did poorly the las' time, so here's yer chance to show 'ow good yer are!

Accuracy today, lads. Yers can all try yer rates o' fire tomorra!"

When he got up to Number Four gun, he looked at me and then at Nobby.

"Nah let's see wot them new sights o' yours will do, Nobby."

"Aye, Johnny." Nobby said in a familiar tone for he and Mr. Johns were old mates. "I'm reckon thart we'll split 'ere in twain an' that's no bilge!"

"See that yer do, matey. The Cap'n givin a crown to the crew wot does it, bless 'is heart!"

The night before, I had fashioned the rear sight and had fixed it to the end of the flintlock mechanism at the rear of the gun. The foresight was simply a large nail stuck upright in a lump of tar over the centre of the muzzle. It was not expected to last the first shot, so I had made several replacements. I had nailed two small lengths of wood together to form a right angle and had traced out a curved protractor and a plumb bob to make up the rest of elevation scale. My rough and ready rangefinder was also a makeshift device on which I had calibrated its angles using the same marks which I had put on the protractor. Any gunner could now look through the rangefinder's tubes and obtain a number which would then correspond to those on the protractor. I thought that angles and their sines would be well beyond the average seaman's education.

The helmsman brought the *Thaleia* around before we slowly sailed back to where the target barrel had been thrown overboard. There it was coming up on our side first of all. I quickly checked the approximate range and then put the elevation triangle into the mouth of the gun. Nobby and Taffy gently positioned and tapped the quoin at the gun's rear whilst I motioned with my hand to raise the gun up. Up, up, stop. Down went my hand and I retracted the elevation triangle. The gun had been loaded before we had come about so Nobby was ready at the rear sight.

Guns Numbers One to Three had fired and whilst their aims seemed to be better than the previous exercise, no shot had yet hit the barrel. Now it was our turn.

"Steady, cumon nah! Jest a little. Cum'n inta view.'
Nobby was saying quietly to himself as the target
began to appear in our gunport. Nobby pulled the
lanyard.

'Thundering Tilly' fired with the usually amount of
flame and smoke and jerked backwards. Before the
smoke cleared there came a loud cheer from the deck
above. As the smoke cleared, we saw only some
smoke and fragments on the water where the target
barrel had been. Success!

Mr Johns suddenly appeared behind us.

"Well done, lads. That'l be a ginea for yer, mates!
We've must be alookin' at them sights o' yers, now
if'n they can do thart!"

We looked at each other, faces covered in soot from
the powder and big grins on our faces. A crown!
That was a very large amount of money, even split
by six men! That was my last thought, however. I
was mighty pleased with myself that a little
twentieth-century technology, nineteenth if I was
honest with myself, could make such a major
difference. I finally felt that my education had finally

added something to the lives of my shipmates. Later that day, I was again rewarded when Mr. Johns came back and asked me for the plans of my sights and the mock-up of his elevation triangle. He gave me a wink and said:

"I'll see Mr. Wilks, the Armourer abart these. I'm think'n that we could knock up sump'n a might permanent like and fit 'em to the rest o' the long guns. What yer think, Jenkins?"

"Thankee, Mr. Johns. That's to my likin'" I said knuckling my forehead and feeling every inch a member of the *Thaleia*'s crew.

The Captain was most pleased with the rest of the exercise as no other gun had hit the second target which the Bos'n had prepared, fearing the worst. Our crown was brought down by our Divisional Officer, Mr. FitzAdam with the Captain's compliments. Mr. FitzAdam stayed a while and asked me how I had made the gun sights and how I had matched them to the elevation triangle. As he was a man of some education in mathematics, I explained the basic trigonometry which went into my calculations.

"Well, I'll be dashed, Jenkins!" he exclaimed when I had finished. "I know a little bit of trigonometry, meself, but those calculations are beyond me. I still have trouble remembering how to get those jolly sine, cosine and tangent things when I need's them."

We had restored and secured the gun and lowered our mess table for the next meal, but the rest of my mates had wandered off to brag about their gunnery and no doubt get a 'wet' from some of the other gun crew who always had a bottle or two hidden away for just such an occasion. As Mr. FitzAdam and I were now alone, I felt that perhaps I could help him with his problem.

"Look, sir. It's simply a matter of learning the basics and then doing some practice." I said, taking a few sheets of paper from our little store. I drew up two right-angle triangles onto the page; one having two 45^0 angles and the other having 30^0 and 60^0 angles. I reminded Mr. FitzAdam of Pythagoras' theorem and gave values for each of the sides of the triangle with a basic value of one for the shortest of the sides.

Thus, I was able then to show him how to find the various trigonometric ratios from an old mnemonic which I had learnt:

'Old Harry Adams Had Old Apples'

Thus, sine was opposite/hypotenuse ('Old/Harry'); cosine was adjacent/hypotenuse ('Adams/Has'); and tangent was opposite/adjacent ('Old/Apples'). Applying the values for the sides of the triangles gave the trigonometrical ratios for sine, cosine and tangent for angles of 30^0, 45^0 and 60^0.

"Well, sink me!" said Mr. FitzAdam. "That's a jolly good way of remembering those trigo things. Me old schoolmaster never did any of that. Just forced me to learn 'em off by heart. Of course, they were forgotten as soon as I walked out of the classroom."

I gave him the sheet of paper with the advice to make many copies so that he would remember these 'trigo things'. I also reminded him that $\sqrt{2}$ was 1.4142 and $\sqrt{3}$ was 1.7320 but as he had confessed to poor memory, showed him how to estimate square roots by multiplying same numbers, so that 1.4 multiplied by itself gave 1.96 and so on. Later, in another session I showed him how to derive the values for the trigonometrical functions for other angles as values between known functions such as for sines where that of zero degrees was zero, so all sines between angles of zero degrees and thirty degrees would be I increments of about 0.0174 per degree, as zero to thirty represented 29 steps from zero to one half.

To young Mr. FitzAdam, such elementary trigonometry was a revelation and he resolved to write out my little sheet once every night until he could confidently learn it by heart. He had also noticed that I kept a diary and enquired how I used it; he had never thought of keeping one himself. I explained that it helped me remember all of the useful and interesting things which went on daily in a sailor's life and that one day it may be interesting to my descendants.

"What a capital idea, Jenkins!" he exclaimed. "We Middies must keep our logbooks, of course, but they are for the more formal running of the ship. A diary! Well, now that is a good idea. I will start one as soon as I can get a small book from the Purser this afternoon. An' I'll put your trigo lessons in first up!"

With another new found idea, Mr Midshipman FitzAdam went away happy.

It had been another interesting morning at sea, my shipmates were pleased with their success and Mr. FitzAdam was now more confident with his trigonometry; a vital please of study for his navigational training and with the resolve to record his daily life for all of the FitzAdams yet to come.

The *Thaleia* now encountered the usual Westerlies as we rounded the island of Ushant headed southeast into the Bay of Biscay. Our blockade station, according to Mr. FitzAdam's useful intelligence was to be along the French coastline between Brest and Saint-Nazaire, although Brest was the most important and a well-known ship-building harbour. He also confided that the waters to the east of Ushant were particularly dangerous now that we were on a lee shore and we could be pushed onto land by the westerly winds.

Luckily, our captain and the ship's Master, 'Jock' McInnes, had no intention of being wrecked on the coast of France and kept well away from both Ushant and the mainland by good seamanship. Our days thus became routine and boring; broken only by changes in the weather and the need for continual changes of sail. Hearing 'all hands on deck to shorten sail' was a common event, usually in the small hours of the night when the wind seemed to take on a perverse and personal nature to increase in its fury.

It was well into our third week of blockade duty when Scrounger came to our mess table with the news that old Purvis, the Captain's Clerk had suddenly died. Considering the many risks on board a frigate in such a stormy part of the world, simply dying of old age was not a common event. Henry Purvis, I was told had been a school master in his day and like me, had been in the wrong place at the wrong time when the Press arrived. He had been with the captain for many years and now was to be buried at sea away from the green hills of England.

There was no Bos'n's call nor beating of the drums in this ship for a burial service. The word was quickly passed around with the muffled cry of:

"All hands bury the dead, ahoy!" and all hands except those involved with running the ship assembled on the gun deck where the service was to be conducted.

Captain Trevallyn was in his full-dress uniform with a black band around his arm. Having no Chaplin aboard, he was the one who conducted all of the church services, including burials at sea. He and the other officers except the Officer-of-the-Watch had come forward and now stood near the open gangway. Captain Spotswood stood at the end of a small line of his Marines who waited silently as usual with their muskets by their side. The body of poor Henry Purvis was tightly wrapped in his canvas hammock which now served as his shroud. He was laid upon a plank which had its end at the gangway. Mr. Bosanquet, the First Officer, solemnly draped the Union flag over the body and fastened the ends at the other end of the plank.

Watching these simple proceedings gave me time to think about another aspect of life, or here, death at sea. Death is at all times is a sad event, but never so much so as at sea. There is a suddenness when a man dies at sea and a difficulty for his shipmates to realise it. On a ship, even a small one like a frigate, men are shut up together upon the endless sea. For months on end they see no other vista but the sea and the sky; and their own little ship amongst it. Taken suddenly from among them, they will remember their shipmate in many little vignettes; his presence at the mess table, the sound of his laughter at play; and his cries in the storm and battle. And there are rarely any new shipmates to fill an empty berth and one man wanting when the night watch is mustered and thoughts drifting home are abroad.

Henry Purvis was an old man by anyone's standard. The Captain's Clerk, was somewhat like myself, being different from the rest of the crew, and had led a relatively solitary life onboard the *Thaleia* and the other ships which Captain Trevallyn had commanded. None the less, he had made some friends on the *Thaleia*; he had messed in the Petty Officer's Mess and of course, shared some friendship of a kind with the captain. In this, there had always been the formal relationship between captain and servant, but there were many private instances when the captain would have to share correspondence which was often dictated to his clerk with the feelings which often went with it. A ship's captain's life is a lonely life.

Prior to taking the body to the gangway, members of his mess, probably the senior Petty Officers, would have removed the old man's clothes, washed his body and then the Sailmaker would have stitched it up in the dead man's own hammock. I had read that there was supposed to be a tradition whereby the last stitch went through the nose of the deceased to ensure that he really had died but there was no mention of it here. One or two nine-pounder shot would have been placed in the shroud at the foot of the corpse to weight it down when it was cast into the sea.

Now on deck, the flag-covered corpse lay on the deck ready for its departure from the ship, his home and friends. Captain Trevallyn and all assembled, except Captain Spotswood and his Marines, had removed their hats and the captain opened his Book of Common Prayer to read the short service, finishing with the well-known lines:

"We therefore commit his body to the deep, to be turned into corruption, looking for the resurrection of the body when the sea shall give up her dead, and the life of the world to come, through our Lord Jesus Christ; who at his coming shall change our vile body, that it may be like his glorious body, according to the mighty working, whereby he is able to subdue all things to himself. Amen."

The Marines raised their muskets to their shoulders and fired a single volley. Two seamen delegated to the task, lifted up the head end of the plank and the mortal remains of Henry Purvis slid from under the flag he had served so quietly into the sea.

"Caps on!" shouted the Master-at-Arms and the crew turned and went about their business. The officers replaced their caps and went about their duties or to their wardroom. It was over. It was though nothing had happened and nothing remained of Henry Purvis on the ship except a few memories.

Later in the Petty Officer's Mess, the few belongings which poor Henry had possessed would be auctioned with a view of sending the money to his family. But poor Henry had no family as anyone could recall and so there was no auction of his few belongings and so his cheap and battered pocket watch, his small Bible and his clothing were shared amongst his few friends.

After our evening meal, I sat down with the rest of my mess at our table over the great gun. There had been silence as we ate; there was none of the camaraderie which usually accompanied our meals. Nobby, who had explained the procedure of burial at sea to me, pulled down the black bottle from its well-known hiding place and lifted down the six tin mugs from their hooks. He poured a little of the strong sprit into each of the mugs.

"Well, Lads, I's time fo' a wet for pur ol' 'Arry Purvis. A gud man, I'm told, an' he'll be mis'd by 'is mates an' all. Cheers!"

"'An tha' cap'in too!" said Scrounger Smith who often had 'dealings' with the late clerk when supplies of paper and ink were needed for letters home. As the sun was setting through the clouds over a rolling grey sea, all was quiet on the *Thaleia* except the wind through the rigging and the occasional flap of a loose sail.

It came somewhat of a shock to me when Mr. FitzAdam interrupted our breakfast the next morning. It was his early morning rounds of course, when he would walk down the long gun deck hatless and with his boyish smile on his face. This morning he stopped at our table and with a solemn look on his face said in a formal tone.

"Come with me, Jenkins. The Captain wants to see you."

I looked around at my messmates, they looked back just as stunned as I was; it was uncommon for a captain to summon a lowly sailor, especially at breakfast. All I could do was to stand, put on my cloth cap and offer a meek 'yes, sir' to the young Midshipman as he turned and walked on to the stern below the Quarterdeck where the Captain's cabins were located.

We walked through the gun deck, past the mizzen mast and the stern companionway which led up to the Quarterdeck and to the vestibule at the door to the Captain's quarters. Mr. FitzAdam replaced his hat as the marine at the door gave him a non-committal salute with his arm swinging sharply across his musket.

The young Midshipman knocked at the door and received a firm reply:

"Come!" The voice of the captain was both firm and devoid of any emotion.

Mr. FitzAdam opened the door and removed his hat.

"Landsman Jenkins, sir." he said nervously. Midshipmen rarely went to the Captain's cabin at such an hour. He ushered me into the presence of the great man himself.

"Thank you, Mr. FitzAdam. That will be all;" said the captain allowing the young Midshipman to quietly withdraw and close the door behind him.

"Come forward, Jenkins. I won't bite you." The captain said with a smile on his face. He was seated at a large desk which seemed to occupy far end of the cabin which took up most of the upper stern of the ship; the dim light of the early morning trying feebly to come through the stern windows which formed the rear wall of the cabin.
I took a few tentative steps towards the desk; my cloth cap being wrung into tight knots in my hands. I would have to be cautious here. The captain was not only a well-educated man by eighteenth-century standards but had the reputation amongst the crew

as being observant and possessed of a quick intelligence.

"Stand easy, Jenkins. You are not in trouble. Indeed, I need your help!" the captain said looking up from the book which he had open on the desk in front of him.

"I see by the Ship's Roll that you were a bookbinder's apprentice before you were pressed. Am I correct in assuming that you can read and write?"

"Yes sir." I replied quietly and with little enthusiasm. This will be a good test of my assumed identity I thought.

"Any Latin or Greek?" the captain asked.

"No sir, just the basic education at the Parish school." I replied, trying awfully hard to imagine just what a 'bookbinder's apprentice' did to get the job.

"Well never mind. As long as you can pen a good hand and read long, boring missives from the

Admiralty, that is what I need for the moment. I have you in mind as my clerk. Will you take on this task?"

I thought for a moment. My education as a simple tar and gunner so far had been an eye-opener to me about the life of a sailor in the eighteenth-century and my entries each night in my little diary would be most handy to Fitzy's studies when I returned to my own time. Suddenly here was an opportunity to go 'behind the scenes' as it were, to learn more of how such a ship was commanded and sailed.

"Thankee sir." I said knuckling my bare forehead. "That is a great opportunity."

The captain gave a short laugh and stood up. The deckhead above us was low and, being a tall man, he had to stoop a little as he walked around and opened a side door to a small cabin beyond.

"You may not think so in time Jenkins, for I can be a crusty old salt at times and I may need you at any of those times. Of course, this is only a temporary placement until we return to port when I will think about it again."

He opened the side door a little wider.

"This was my former clerk's office. Not much space other than the desk and necessities, but there is some good light through the side windows and the privacy you will need when making copies of my orders and letters to their lordships. Of course, I will require that you keep important issues to yourself. I've been at sea since boyhood, so I know the need for communication aboard a small ship. Sailors will talk, but I will require complete discretion when you are doing your official work; no reading documents like you probably did as an apprentice."

"No, sir." I replied like a schoolboy being given the school rules.

"As there is little room here, and the Petty Officer's Mess is already a might crowded, I will ask you to continue messing with your gun crew. I am sure that they will like that arrangement as Mr. McAdam has informed me that you seem to get on with Nobby Clarke and his gang of pirates and I will ask Mr. McAdam to find an extra man from the starboard gun deck to assist with Number Four gun when we go into action. Naturally, you will not be required to be on watch but I may need you with me at various odd times to make notes which will assist me in writing up the logbook. Is all of that clear, Jenkins?"

"Fully sir," I replied. It will also give me an opportunity to enter notes into my own little diary with the privacy and opportunity to do so.

The captain resumed his seat behind his desk then looked up and gave than enigmatic smile often seen on his face when things are going as expected.

"Well…good then Jenkins. Square away things with your messmates and report back to me at the end of this Watch. You may go."

"Aye sir, I replied in my best sailor fashion, knuckled my forehead, turned and left the cabin. To my surprise, Mr FitzAdam was waiting for me in the vestibule. The marine standing like some red-painted statue nearby.

"Well, what did the captain want, if I may ask?" he said.

"I'm his new clerk." I said with a grin.

"Oh, I say! What a turn up for the books, Jenkins. Good show…."

He was about to pump me for a few more pieces of information when the captain's voice loudly came through the door.

"Mr FitzAdam! Your presence if you please."

The young Midshipman gave me a nervous look before quickly going through the door. I walked back along the gun deck thinking of how my messmates would take my recent 'promotion' to Captain's Clerk."

"Gud Oh!" said Scrounger. "Nah we'll git tha' scuttlebutt fresh like!"

"Nice job if'n ya can git it." Said Nobby "But nah we've wiffout a gunna! he exclaimed.

I told him of the conversation in regards to my living conditions and that another man would be found from the starboard battery. Nobby sniffed:

"Bunch o' layabou' them starbid gunnas! It'll 'av ta do."

"Well, dat'll give you a grand life, den Tahm!" said Paddy". A sentiment supported by Taffy who simply said.

"Good on yoh, boyoh!"

The young Swede looked up with some despair on his youthful face:

"Ve'll missssen you und yourren helplpen vidden our lettennrs."

"Never mind, lads." I said with some jocularity." You aren't rid of me yet. I'll be around for scran and the odd talk. Just you see. I will always be here to help with your letters, Swede."

So now I was the confidante of the captain himself; what new things would I learn about him, his frigate and the men who sailed in her? As I looked out through the open gunport the sea rolled by as it had done since before time itself.

Chapter Nine

The *Trinity*

My duties as Captain's Clerk were not arduous, they were mostly to do with making written copies of orders for the officers. On our distant blockade duty of the rugged Brittany coastline, there was not much correspondence for me to receive, file nor to take dictation for its reply. Old Purvis had long since devised a filing system in the oaken chest of drawers which were kept in the small cabin. There was also a good supply of pens, ink and paper and time for me to commit my thoughts and observations to my diary.

Not going on watch was a blessing; no more being woken by a rough shake of my hammock in the middle of the night, putting on every stitch of clothing that I possessed and then borrowed oils to go out into the cold, wild, windy and wet blackness of the heeling, slippery deck that is a ship in a turbulent ocean. The ship carried our small lights, of course, but their dim glow was more for someone at a distance, not the poor souls who have to negotiate their way around the deck or even claw up the ratlines to capture a loose sail. One has to always protect one's night vision I was often told by the others in my watch, but looking out through the sea spray and wind into the darkness beyond gave little fear of that.

Blockade duty, despite all of the romanticism of the novels by such great authors as Forester, O'Brian and Kent, was mostly boredom interspersed with small emergencies and odious tasks. Securing loose sails and sheets swabbing the decks, oiling the woodwork and the occasional homely duties of feeding the ship's livestock and cleaning below decks occupied most of our time when not on watch. There were the usual inconveniences of trying to eat on a table with the ship rolling this way then that and sleeping in a wet hammock fully clothed. Our days became simply a matter of tedium with the usual duties and work parties needed to operate a square-rigged ship at sea.

We had been at sea now for several weeks, there had been little action save the sighting of neutral ships which were investigated, some small traders out of

France which were captured and sent back home with a few men as Prize Crew and rarely an occasional French frigate or sloop-of-war which we would chase back to Brest, Saint-Nazaire or one of the other smaller French ports.

The most exciting events were the several gunnery practices which the captain insisted upon. He had not been happy with our initial drill and so was prepared to deplete his own supply of powder to increase our rate of fire. For me, it was exciting to watch my old gun team perform the actions which they relished. The big eighteen-pounder was loaded with a bag of gunpowder which the Swede had brought up from the magazine. Next a wad of old rope was rammed down the barrel to prevent the charge from falling out. Then the ball was pushed in and rammed home followed by another wad to prevent it rolling back out. The crew would then pull on the tackles which 'ran out the gun' so that its muzzle was well out of the open gun port. Lastly, Nobby the Gun Captain would prick the powder charge bag with his quill and reset the flintlock mechanism in place with its flint in place and its hammer cocked. With a loud cry of "stand clear!" he would pull the lanyard which fired the gun. The gun was then swabbed out with the long pole and its wet swab to ensure that there were no sparks left inside the barrel. Then the sequence would start all over again. By the end of the last session of drill, the *Thaleia's* gun crews could fire a round every two minutes; considered a very rapid rate of fire indeed.

Some days were fine with the sun appearing for short periods; clothing and bedding were dried and the men set about repairing any damage done the night before. I still messed with my friends at Number Four gun larboard but I missed their companionship after dinner as my day as a clerk often went well into the night and with the captain's dispensation, I was able to go down to the galley and get what food was left over. 'Slushy' Watson was a good-natured individual unlike many cooks whom my shipmates had complained about on other ships. There seemed to be a standard ritual whenever the topic of sea cooks came up:

"Who called the cook a bastard?" would come as a mock officer's cry in an effeminate high-pitched voice from one of our number, usually Taffy Evens who gave the ineffectual enquiry a lovely Welsh lilt.

"Who called the bastard a cook?" would come the chorus of all of the others in reply. This would be followed by much laughter and yet another story would emerge of some dreaded 'dough-puncher' that one of the mess had once encountered.

'Slushy' Watson was neither a bastard nor a simple 'dough-puncher'; he was a happy soul who took his profession seriously exhibiting great pride in being able to feed two hundred or so souls; especially on board a frigate which usually rolled in any sort of a sea and where food items were often wet with the ubiquitous seawater which trickled down throughout the ship. His stores were supplied by the Victualling Board and were for the most part, salted down in barrels or stored dried in bags and canisters. Fresh food brought on board at the start of the cruise usually did not last long and items such as milk from the ship's cow or goat and eggs from its hens were usually used only for the officer's table; assuming that these poor creatures survived their hazardous life at sea for any length of time.

Like many ships' cooks, 'Slushy' was a former Greenwich Pensioner who had been hospitalised out from the navy after losing part of one leg below the knee. To him, this had been an advantage as he could still get around on his wooden leg and keep out of the usual dangers of being on deck. Still, he kept long hours and had to contend with the grumbles and adverse comments of his shipmates.

He was also in luck in having a captain who was well up on the needs to sustain a healthy crew and a purser who was not totally corrupt and who also shared these modern notions. Apart from the usual regulation bulk food items supplied by the Victualling Board, there were items carried in smaller quantities or 'purser's necessaries' included almonds, barley, currants, garlic, mace, nutmeg, rice, sago, shallots, sugar, and various fruits and vegetables when they could be obtained. He also had a good supply of lemons, the juice of which was issued to a reluctant crew for the prevention of scurvy, an act which had only been recently introduced to the important rituals of the navy. Even with his limitations, 'Slushy' managed to provide a hot meal daily, with meat four times a week, together with bread, cheese and small beer with fresh vegetables and fruit from time to time. Though it was generally lacking in vitamins, this ration was more than adequate and it could be said that sailors ate significantly better than most of those people ashore. I found that in time, I could always count on some hot salted beef stew and a mug of warm grog and the warmth of 'Slushy's big oven in his galley late at night. He had his hammock rigged not far away and there was always a cask or two for sitting on and chatting in front of the stove.

It was another cold, blustery day with the usual westerly winds blowing in from the Atlantic as we headed southward through an indifferent grey sea, on a starboard reach. I was up on the Quarterdeck attending the captain who wished to dictate some details about the ship's handling which he would later put into an official letter, when the hail from aloft came.

"Da ya hear tha'! Sail abaft on the starboard beam!"

Captain Trevallyn looked out to starboard and called for a telescope. This was offered by Mr. Bosanquet, the First Officer who had just come up on deck.

"She's a bigg'un, Mr. Bosanquet! A Don by the look of the shape of her skysails. What do you think?" he said, handing the telescope back to the younger officer.

"She's a Don alright, sir. And I think that there's a smaller ship behind on her larboard side. She's got her mains set and seems to be in a hurry. Heeled right over, she is."

The captain retrieved the telescope and took another look at the two ships coming up on our stern some distance away.

"Well. Nothing to do yet until we see what their intentions are. The Dons have joined the French so we cannot think that they will have friendly intentions." He turned to me and said:

"Jenkins, note down that at just after six bells in the Morning Watch, we did sight two sail coming from the north by northwest. Then go below and get our last position and its time from the chart."

"Aye, sir." I replied and made a note in my day book.

The captain again turned to his First Lieutenant and said:

"You had better alert the Master, the Bos'n and the Master Gunner, Mr. Bosanquet. We may have some work for the guns this day. In the meantime, we will just have to wait and see what ensues."

The weather seemed to be calming a little and after obtaining our last position, I took a detour past Number Four Gun where my shipmates were squaring their mess away after breakfast.

"Two ships some way off our stern." I said with some concern.

"Aye, mate. We'um heard tha' cry frum tha' mast'ed. Frenchies,'re they? Asked Nobby.

"Not certain yet, but the captain thinks that one is a 'big Don."

"Ah! A big Don, is she?" Nobby replied with a grin. "They's lik' ta mak'em big, doo tha' Spanish. We cud be 'eaded fo' a dustup, then!"

I quickly left to find the chart near the wheel below the Quarterdeck, but I did not particularly like Nobby's anticipation of a 'dustup' with a 'big Don'. We were only a frigate of thirty-eight guns and not a ship-of-the-line designed to fight such big ships.

Unlike the movies of such possible action, tall ships took considerable time to get into fighting position, so I was going to have plenty of time to observe our preparations. The Master, the Bos'n, the Master Gunner, Captain Spotswood and the First and Second Lieutenants had all come up with the captain. There was a trace of concern on his face and he looked around his most important officers.

"They have the weather gauge on us gentlemen and they mean business. We are on a lee shore, so I'm guessing that they will either catch us and blow us out of the water or drive us ashore on the Brittany coast. Neither is of my liking."

It was then that Mr. FitzAdam came rushing up full of youthful excitement, his telescope waving in the air:

"Sir, sir, she' the *Nuestra Señora de la Santísima Trinidad*, Captain!" he exclaimed. "I saw her in Cadiz when I was there during the peace. She carries 140 guns on three decks with thirty-six and twenty-four pounders. She'll blow us to pieces!"

"Yes, thank you Mr. FitzAdam. Please resume your duties," replied the captain with huge sangfroid.

He turned back to his small group of officers and spoke. "Well, there we have it, gentlemen. The *Trinity* will be upon us if we are not careful. We certainly cannot out-gun her, and we also have a French frigate to deal with. Our best hope is to try and outrun them both. We still have some sea-room, so I intend to keep on this course for a while to get further west then we will head south by southwest and try to outrun them"

I listened to this conversation with the utmost intensity. Something was in the back of my mind about this impending action. It was something which I had remembered from some years ago when I was reading a book on the history of the 'Days of fighting Sail when I was relaxing after a tedious bout with Schrödinger's wave equation. Then I heard the captain mention the name 'Trinity'.

Of course! 'Trinity Trevallyn' was what the newspapers of the day had called our captain after the brilliant action against the *Trinity* and the French 40-gun frigate, the *Aèteia* in the Bay of Biscay in this very year.

However, it now looked like history was going to be changed and we would be lost as the two ships seemed to be gaining upon us. It was most likely that our hopes to outrun them would not be successful. I had not considered that by travelling back in time to simply observe history that I would now be forced into making it happen. I did the unthinkable as a simple member of the crew and approached the captain and his group of officers.

"Sir! Please forgive my intrusion," I said with some excitement and a little fear. "I know that I am but a simple landsman, but I could not help to observe that the big ship yonder is well tilted over. Surely some of her lower gun ports will be closed and will not be able to bear upon us. Her other guns would also have to be highly elevated to put a broadside across the sea instead of into it at long range."

The captain looked at me with some patience whilst the others stood back in some distaste that a member of the crew should approach the captain on his own Quarterdeck and tell him what to do. Captain Trevallyn did not reply but grabbed a telescope from his First Lieutenant and looked at the ships off our stern; first at the Trinity and then at the French frigate.

He handed the telescope back to his First and gave me a very quizzical look. He turned back to the others and said:

"Belay my last order! We will continue this course until they get closer." He turned to Mr. Unger the Bos'n: "Tell some of your best topmen to dither a little whilst getting the extra sails bent on. I intend to have those ships catch up to us."

The other officers looked about in some form of disbelief and Mr. Bosanquet spoke up:

"But sir, the Trinity will blow us all into splinters if she catches us!"

"I intend that she will catch us, Mr. Bosanquet, but I think that the splinters will be elsewhere."

The captain moved over to the stern taffrail and pointed.

"You see, gentlemen? The *Trinity* is heeled right over. Her lower gun ports will be closed and her other guns will probably still be set at the usual low angle. Knowing the Don's gunnery, they will probably not be too well elevated at any rate. Her gunners will take some time to elevate their guns so that their shot will probably hit the water before they find our range. If we're lucky, we will take them both by surprize." He said with some enthusiasm. Then he pointed a little way over towards the French frigate:

"Now, look at the French frigate. She is also heeled right over and her guns will be pointing too high. I intend to go about and head directly to cross the bows of the Don. If I'm right, she will turn a few

points and that will put her further over. Then..."
and here the captain turned to the Bos'n again:

" ...we will go about...smartly, Mr. Unger and cross
over close to the Frenchie. I intend to rake her and
dismast the *Trinity* as we pass between them. They
may even be afeared to shoot at risk of hitting each
other. Now gentlemen, I'm sure that you will know
what to do, so go about your duties."

The captain turned to me and gave me another of his
dark looks with one eyebrow well elevated. In a
quiet voice he said:

"Thankee for that, Mr. Jenkins. It will get a might hot
up here later; you may return to your duties below
if you wish."

"Aye, sir" I replied as there was little more that I
could say now that I had set history back on its
proper course. I went down the ladder and to my
mates on Number Four gun larboard. Mr. Johns, the
Master Gunner was already on the gun deck. Like
the other officers, he knew his trade and how to turn
the captain's wishes into orders for his gun crews.
He was walking down past each gun telling them

what to load and to set their sights high. There would be little time to find the range as we would be quickly changing our position relative to the two other ships. Whilst on deck, Mr. McInnes the Master, had used his sextant to estimate the current distance between the two ships and, assuming that we would swing over to about one third of that distance to close with the Frenchman, he had given the Master Gunner the approximate ranges for both starboard and larboard guns.

The larboard guns had the task of dismasting the Spaniard. This would be done with both chain shot and round shot; the chain shot consisting of two halves of a hallow ball joined by a length of chain would cut the standing rigging and sails, the round shot could be fired with greater accuracy and would be aimed at the base of the mainmast. Number Four gun was to be loaded with round shot and Nobby had the gun elevated to the appropriate angle. The following ships would be ill-prepared, but we were ready for action.

Chapter Ten

Beat to Quarters!

It seemed an eternity watching the two enemy ships slowly catching up to us. The crew of the *Thaleia* went about their business as usual, except the topmen who were making a great show of mishandling the sails much to the joy of the deckhands who yelled friendly comments of derision at them.

The captain had been watching the approaching ships and also looking up at the tell-tails which showed the direction of the wind. He motioned to the Bos'n:

"Prepare to go about, Mr. Unger," he said quietly.

The Bos'n knuckled his forehead and then took up his speaking trumpet and went to the railing of the Quarterdeck.

"Hands to the halyards. Prepare to go about!" he yelled.

"Execute!" said the captain and the two Quartermaster Assistants on the big wheel spun it round so that the ship turned about with enough momentum to pass through the eye of the wind and on to its new course with the wind now on a close reach heading for the *Trinity*. The mechanisms of sailing a sailing vessel of some size appealed to my love of physics and I could not help but marvel at the natural control which the captain and his crew now exercised to bring the *Thaleia* on what seemed a collision course with the big Spaniard.

No doubt there would be some panic aboard both the *Trinity* and the French frigate; they would not expect their trapped prey to turn upon them. As expected, the *Trinity* changed her course a point or two to starboard, bringing her abeam of the wind and causing her to heel further over with such a large expanse of sail. The Frenchman also altered course slightly to keep abreast of the bigger ship.

The Captain Trevallyn hoped that the *Trinity*'s captain would think that we were trying to slip past at significant relative speed by tacking into the wind and so escape to westward. We were all gratified when we saw the starboard gun ports of the *Trinity* open, for we were soon to do another manoeuvre and turn on a broad reach across the *Trinity*'s bow to head directly for the Frenchman.

"We'll give her a broadside as we pass!" the captain called down to the Master Gunner, now standing on the gun deck anticipating such an order. This was now a test for our larboard guns who would need to reload in a hurry.

We crossed the *Trinity*'s bow at an extreme range for our eighteen-pounders which had been set at a high angle and loaded with alternative chain and round shot.

"Fire as you bear!" yelled the Master Gunner and our guns fired one after the other. The Spaniards had been caught unawares and so answering shot came from their bow guns. I watched with some fascination as their guns wreaked havoc with the Spaniard's jibs, foresails and their stays and splintered their bowsprit rigging.

"Gud shootin', lads!" the Master Gunner yelled as he strode along the walkway above the open section of the gun deck.

"Nah, load up 'an aim fur 'er foremast. I'm thinkin' that e'm be a might weak, nah!"

I watched as Nobby and his crew reloaded Number Four gun with ball; alternative crews loaded with chain shot. We were rapidly moving away from the *Trinity* and heading now for the Frenchman. Our larboard eighteens fired again with a loud succession of deep booms; the smaller nines on the quarter deck adding to the cacophony as they also fired. There were a few shots fired from some of the guns on the upper two decks of the *Trinity*, but they had only just been run out and the guns had not yet been accurately aimed.

The Frenchman came up fast on our starboard quarter, her gun ports open. She was going to give as good as she got, but we all hoped that her guns were elevated too high as her hull still heeled over away from us.

Our starboard guns were elevated at their maximum height loaded with grape shot and canister and our devastating cannonades were also loaded with canister. Our tactics were to sweep the Frenchman's deck with murderous shot and kill as many of the crew as possible. The close-quarter battle with the Frenchman raged on our starboard side whilst the larboard gunners purposely aimed at the rigging and foremast of the Spaniard.

We were now taking shot ourselves; there would be an occasional thud as a ball would strike the hull and but cause little damage which the Carpenter and his mates would rush to repair. Mostly the shot from the Frenchman's high-angled guns would pass overhead and through the rigging. Sails were holed and there were high-pitched twangs as round shot hid our standing rigging. Occasionally, some piece of rigging such as loose blocks and cordage would cascade down onto the netting which had been set across the open gun deck. Thankfully the French had not anticipated our manoeuvres and had not loaded with chain nor canister. The *Trinity* fired several ragged broadsides at us but most of the badly-aimed shot fell short or bounced over the water to strike our solid lower hull.

There was a loud cheer from the larboard gunners and I ran out onto the open gun deck and climbed part of the way up the larboard Quarterdeck ladder just in time to see the foremast of the *Trinity* come crashing down over her starboard side, taking its sails and rigging along with it. It now acted like a giant sea-anchor causing the *Trinity* to swing violently around and heel further over as the wind now came behind her remaining sails. She had come to a halt, dead in the water.

I had once delighted in watching movie dramatization of battles at sea in the swash-buckling movies such as *Captain Blood* and *Horatio Hornblower* but it was a different feeling actually being in one. Fear was the greatest emotion, along with a strong sense of self preservation. Below, on the gun deck, there was a pandemonium of noise and action all wreathed in a strong, dark veil of acrid gunpowder smoke. The gun crews had trained for this and had experienced battle before. They went about their methodical work in the midst of all of this chaos but fear still lurked in the heart of every man. There was a crash and cries above the turmoil as a ball from the Frenchman smashed its way through the hull, killing and wounding several of Number Six gun.

The younger boys of the gun crews ran to fetch more powder or shot or splash tubs of water on to any spark which had come from a fired gun. Others threw copious handfuls of sand onto the deck to prevent slippage on the water and the blood which had started to flow across the deck.

Some men helped to move the dead and wounded away from operating guns; the wounded to be taken below by the 'loblolly boys' and the dead to be passed through a gun port and thrown overboard. The wounded were carried down to the Petty Officer's wardroom which was now a makeshift surgery where our surgeon, Mr. Cunningham carried his bloody duties of removing large splinters or amputating limbs.

We passed the side of the Frenchman with some speed and our carronades and nine-pounders had extracted a huge toll of dead and wounded upon our enemy's deck. I had been summoned back to the Quarterdeck were the captain wished to dictate a few brief notes on the encounter so far. The Quarterdeck was often the main target for enemy sharpshooters and their smaller cannon. Mr. Jamison the Third Officer was lying on the deck being attended to my one of the Midshipman. He had taken a musket ball though his shoulder and looked deathly pale. Our wheel had several spokes shot away and one of the two quartermasters was lying on the deck in a large pool of blood. Captain Spotswood, as dapper as usual was directing a line of his marines who were keeping the French sharpshooters down as well as directing some of their own volleys towards the French Quarterdeck which now seemed remarkably empty.

"Extra training value!" he said, turning to me with a smile after a musket ball had taken away his shako. He stooped and picked it up, a protruding finger through the neat round hole just near its top.

Captain Trevallyn stood calmly on his deck, looking at the destruction his carronades were causing on the French ship. He looked up at the tell-tales fluttering from one of the mizzen backstays.

"Prepare to come about, Mr Unger. We will rake his stern as we pass." The captain said in a firm voice to the Bos'n who was standing across the deck. He then walked to the railing and looked down at the Master Gunner who had been walking the gun deck giving instruction and encouragement to his gunners. "Have the starboard guns and carronades load with round shot. We will take out his stern, if you please."

To fire a broadside at very close range through another ship's stern was the ultimate act of devastation. There was little protection inside down the length of a ship, especially one the size of a frigate, as most of the bulkheads or interior walls were simple partitions which were usually removed before battle. This meant that any shot taken through the stern windows of the ship would pass down its length doing utmost damage.

"Fire as ya bear!" came the coarse yell from Mr. Johns to his starboard gun crew.

The guns fired off in succession and I watched in horror as the beautiful ornate stern of the French ship with its tall windows of small panes disintegrated piece by piece. The destruction inside the ship would have been tremendous. I had but a fleeting glimpse of the name of the French frigate high up on its transom as we passed; *Aèteia*.

"Look sir!" shouted Mr. Bosanquet, the First Officer in some excitement and pointing away from the action. "The *Trinity* is bearing away!"

Everyone on the Quarterdeck turned from the Frenchman and looked out over through the smoke to where we had left the *Trinity* wallowing in the sea. Her crew had been able to cut away the shrouds and general rigging which had been taken over her side when her foremast had fallen. She had reset her sails on the remaining two masts and was now heading away from the battle, leaving her French escort to her fate.

"She's running for Saint-Nazaire, I'll wager," said old 'Jock' McInnes, the Master who had been standing near the ship's wheel.

"She's struck, God bless us!" said Captain Spotswood, pointing back to the *Aèteia* which had hauled down its flag and backed her remaining tattered sails so that she would come to a stop.

"Bring her about, Mr Unger and put us up along the Frenchman's side." The captain said to the Bos'n.

"Boarding party, if you please Mr. Bosanquet and your marines Captain Spotswood."

Both men turned and gave a quick doff of their hats to the captain and then quickly walked off to organise the boarding parties which would board the *Aèteia*, where Mr. Bosanquet would take her captain's surrender.

Chapter Eleven

Time to go Home

"Attend me if you will, Jenkins." The captain said as he left the Quarterdeck and went down the companionway to his cabin. Once inside, he closed the door and sat down at his desk.

"You trouble me, Jenkins!" he said in a concerned tone. "I owe you much for your suggestion about the *Trinity's* position but I cannot resolve such a suggestion coming from a humble bookbinder's apprentice. Moreover, there is the matter of your trigonometry lessons given to Mr. FitzAdam and the innovative gunsights which Mr. John's has been bragging about. Who are you really?"

I had feared this day, hoping that I could continue my subterfuge as simply Tom Jenkins, bookbinder's apprentice and pressed landsman. I should have been aware that such an astute man as Captain Trevallyn would tumble to my identity sooner or later. We in modern times tend to look back through our scantily-written history books and think of people of past years as lacking our intelligence simply because their world was not as technical as ours. We sometimes marvel in a naively innocent way when we discover some ancient technique or writing which suggests that our forefathers had all of the capabilities of thought which we possess.

I stood before the captain like some errant schoolboy who had just been caught stealing apples in the squire's orchard. I knew that I could no longer continue my deception.

"If I told you the truth of my story, Captain Trevallyn, you would have been clapped in irons as a madman until I could be taken to Bedlam."

The captain gave me a quizzical look, raising one eyebrow and replied:

"Well, now Jenkins – if that is your real name – I promise to give you a fair hearing and I will not have you clapped in irons. That is, unless you are a wanted criminal and then I even might make some allowances for your help. So, sit you down and tell me your tale."

I walked over to one of the chairs in the cabin and sat down. After some time and a few deep breaths, I began my tale.

"My name is not Jenkins, as you have surmised and I was never a bookbinder's apprentice. I concocted that part of my story so that I would better fit into this part of the world and its time."

There was another long pause and I looked squarely at the captain trying to decide how much of the truth his knowledge and lifestyle could take in. I continued my story, trying to keep it as simple as possible:

"The truth of the matter is that I am Tom Sinclair, a Doctor of Philosophy and Research Student at that university famous for such people as Sir Isaac Newton and I work in the modern version of his old Faculty." I said looking at the captain's face for some sign of suspicion, but he gazed back with a steady eye, his fingertips touching together upon his desk.

"Go on, Dr. Sinclair." He said quietly.

"In my work I had accidently discovered a way to travel in time. Much like this ship can go up and down a river, I found that I could go forward and back along the river of time. My own time is in 1996 and I have come back to your time, two hundred years in the past."

There was no emotion shown on his face as I stated what I had done which would even be difficult for my contemporaries in the Faculty of Physics. I continued:

"I have an interest in this period of history – your time – and so I came back to simply observe the habits and everyday behaviour of the people of Plymouth in what we call the 'days of fighting sail'. My proposed day excursion was unexpectedly interrupted by your Mr. Harris and his Press Gang and so I was taken aboard your ship. I can offer no proof of this and if I gave you any details about your past life then this would be seen as no more than a simple trick that any fairground fortune-teller could spin. Any predictions for your future could be simply an invention"

The captain looked down at the desk in front of him and then lifted up his head until his eyes met mine. There was a hint of sadness on his face.

"Ah, poor Mr. Harris. I'm afraid that he will lead the Press no longer as he was killed in action at the starboard guns." There was another short pause. He stood up and turned to look out of the stern windows of his cabin.

"I accept your story Dr. Sinclair, regardless of its difficulty for a man of my era, but then I am no stranger to the findings of Newton and other men of 'science' as you call our Natural Philosophers. I would not discount the possibility that one day we might travel in time. So, where does that leave you now? he asked with some compassion.

"I'm not sure, Captain Trevallyn." I replied bleakly. "I would need to get back to Plymouth before I could see if I could return to my time. We have been at sea for several months and so my ability to do so is somewhat uncertain."

The captain returned to his desk and sat down. He looked across at me with his enigmatic smile.

"Well, Dr. Sinclair. I think that I can return the great favour that I and the *Thaleia* owe you. We have taken the Frenchman and so when all repairs are made to make her seaworthy again, I will send her back with a prize crew to Plymouth. You can go with her as we in the *Thaleia* still have another few weeks of this blasted blockade before we can return."

I was delighted to hear this good news which would help me begin my long journey back to the future. Then I thought beyond my own predicament:

"Sir, if I may ask another favour of you. There were two men, Jem Jackson and Will Thompson, who were pressed with me. They had just come off an Indiaman and had their Protections yet they were also illegally pressed."

Captain Trevallyn held up his hand and smiled again.

"Whilst the *Thaleia* needs all the hands we can get, I'm sure that I can spare these two men to go with you. I will write you a vague order to allow you and these men to go ashore and I will also dictate to you now three Honourable Discharges which you can write out for yourself and your two friends which I will then sign. I will also have Mr. FitzAdam go with you, and my Coxswain, Howard as well, so there will be no questions asked about your leaving the ship. We don't want any Press Gang hunting for three 'runners' from the *Thaleia*. That would spoil our good reputation, might it not?" he said with a laugh.

He stood up and went to a chest of drawers standing against the hull on one side of his cabin. He pulled out a small box and opened it:

"We owe you a lot…er …Jenkins. So here are five guineas to help you and your mates find a new life ashore. It is not much, but a new start. Now I expect that you had better go and concoct another tall tale to tell your shipboard friends why you are going ashore and not coming back. Perhaps something along the lines which you suggested about 'false impressment' might be in order. It will also cover for the departure of Jackson and Thompson, although the rest of the crew may think of me as a weak captain in doing so."

I took the proffered guineas in my left hand and eagerly shook the captain's hand with the other.

"Thank you with all of my heart, Captain Trevallyn." I said earnestly. "I can assure you that history already knows you to be a fair captain, liked by his crew. It would be unkind to tell a man of the details of his future life, but let me just say that your name and that of the *Thaleia* will go beyond even my time. Thank you."

With that and a feeling of joy and good will, I first sought out Jem and Will who were busy with their Watch repairing the damage to our foc'sle. I quickly told them my invented story that Captain Trevallyn, overjoyed at his victory in a mood of benevolence, had decided to honourably discharge us from his ship. So as not to raise any rumours, they were to only tell their friends that they had been selected as members of the prize crew and that I would give them their papers once we had landed in Plymouth. Naturally they were overjoyed by this and thanked me most heartily.

I went down to Number Four gun where Nobby and his team were busy cleaning up and securing their gun for more sea duty. They had all come through the battle unscathed except poor Swede Larson who now had a bandaged arm where he had taken a wood splinter whilst bringing powder from below.

"E 'as a badge o' 'ahnooehr to show 'is people now!" said Paddy' O'Hanlon with a grin. The Swede looked up at his big friend and gave a weak grimace.

I told them about my impending discharge and whilst there was genuine disappointment that I should be leaving their Mess, they were happy that a 'pressed man' was able to leave with honour.

"Tha's gud noos, matey. We'um be happy fo' ya, but the cap'n will afta git a noo clerk nah, won't 'e?" was all that Nobby could say on behalf of the team.

Scrounger reached up to one of his many secret alcoves high in the hull and brought down an item of scrimshaw, that sailors' art of carving on bone, shell and wood.

"'Ere mate. Sumptin ta remember us wif." He said earnestly and gave me a small, polished piece of bone with a likeness of the *Thaleia* carved into it and its name printed in block letters which he had copied off one of the ship's water pails.

I thanked him and the rest of the mess for their kindness in taking me in and their continued friendship. Friendship and the sincerity which it brings goes beyond time and would always be a natural feature of the human condition.

Later that day, Mr FitzAdam came walking down the gun deck with an apparent lightness in his stride and was even whistling a happy tune.

"Jenkins, Old Fruit!" he said in such a happy voice, using an expression which startled me. "You and I have been selected as part of the prize crew on board the Frenchie. We're going back to good old Plymouth town. What!"

I thanked him and showed all innocence about having my prior knowledge about that posting.

"Mr. Bosanquet, the First will be in command and I am to be his Second! Isn't that good news?" he said with great boyish enthusiasm. "And some more prize money for us all!" he said turning to the gun crew who all knuckled their foreheads and gave various words of thanks.

"I'll expect us to be off by the end of the First Dog Watch, Jenkins, so get all of your kit ready and square up any debts. I'll see you on deck at eight bells." With that, he turned and whistled his way back aft towards his own quarters.

Eight bells came at the end of the First Dog Watch and I took my few possessions, namely the clothes with which I had arrived on board and the guineas, the three discharges and 'vague orders' which the captain had given me in case someone had doubted my going ashore in Plymouth.

I then spent some additional care wrapping my precious diary in a tightly bound tarred canvas bag which was then wrapped several times in oilskin and bound again with tarred cord. I tucked that into an inner pocket of my coat along with the precious papers and guineas.

Captain Trevallyn was eager to part from the *Aèteia* in case the *Trinity* would return with reinforcements or have a change in heart. Just after the eight bells at the end of the First Dog Watch, the prize crew went aboard the *Aèteia* and took over their duties to repair and get the damaged ship underway. The French captain and most of his officers had been killed by the murderous fire of our carronades at our first encounter, and the remaining officers and crew were locked securely below decks. Captain Spotswood had also sent a small detachment of marines on board to maintain security.

Mr. Bosanquet the First Officer, was now our captain and he had sufficient experience and a good chart to get us back to Plymouth, a little over one hundred nautical miles to our northeast. Given the westerly winds and considering the damage to the ship, it would still take us a couple of days to reach our destination.

Three days later, it was another blustery and grey sea day as we hove into Plymouth Sound, sailing up past Mount Edgcumbe and into our anchorage in the Hamoaze. The large Union Jack flying above the French Tricolour on our stern flagstaff would tell all observers that here was yet another good prize for the Royal Navy. The dispatches which Mr. FitzAdam was to take to the Port Admiral would tell the whole story and soon the Royal Mail coach would take the good news to London.

Having anchored and with a substantial amount of work to be done onboard in transferring the French prisoners ashore and continuing the repairs, the Captain Trevallyn's Coxswain Howard, lowered the ships jolly boat and helped Jem, Will and me on board. We had taken our leave of Mr. FitzAdam and Mr. Bosanquet who were also ready to go ashore in the ships launch.

I had taken Mr. FitzAdam aside and thanked him for his kindness whilst I was under his command. He did not know of my true nature and I pressed upon him the importance of maintaining his small diary, telling him that one day his ancestors may like to read of his future adventures at sea.

Jem and Will eagerly took to the oars of the jolly boat and we went ashore to an inconspicuous wharf of Devonport. When we had touched land, Jem and Will stepped ashore but waited until I came forward from the stern sheets of the boat. I asked Howard at the tiller to wait and I went with the two men onto the wharf. Here we said our goodbyes and they were surprised when I told them that I had some business to attend for the captain on the opposite shore at Mount Edgcumbe. They assumed that I meant the big manor house which stood near that high hill. In parting I gave them both one of the guineas from the captain:

"A small compensation from the Captain, mates. Now don't you be goin' near the Minerva again. D'ya hear?"

Jem gave me a self-depreciating grin and replied in an honest voice:

"Well, thankee ta tha' Cap'n. No mate! We've learned our lesson we 'av. And besides, I spied a tall Indioman in the Pool. So's we'm be orf then ta seek a birth in 'er."

With that, he and Will shook my hand before turning up the old wooden wharf to walk back into Plymouth to seek their fortunes again at sea with the Honourable East India Company. They now each had an Honourable Discharge from the Royal Navy, written by myself and signed by Captain Trevallyn, a golden guinea to spend and a good tale to tell of the encounter between the *Thaleia* and the *Nuestra Señora de la Santísima Trinidad.*

I went back to the jolly boat and explained to Howard that the captain wanted me put ashore on the opposite bank.

"Oh aye, Mr Jenkins. The captain telt me thon ye haed tae dae a service for him an thon ye wad be stayin ashore." He said in a broad Scot's accent reminding me of another resourceful man back at my university.

We shoved off and after a while I asked Howard how long he had been with Captain Trevallyn.

"Many y'ars, sir an ah hope tae gae on lookin after the wee man for many more." He said with some pride.

I recalled that Captain Trevallyn went on to have a distinguished career, being knighted for his action against the *Trinity* and capturing the *Aèteia.* Soon the London newspapers will be full of the glorious nature of this action and Captain Trevallyn's knighthood. They would coin the phrase 'Trinity Trevallyn' which would mark him out as one of the most famous of all frigate captains of this age, going on to become an Admiral and a Peer. I needed the captain to have some inkling that the future for him and the *Thaleia* was assured, so I leaned forward and said to Howard:

"Captain Trevallyn and his ship will become famous and I would not be surprised if you go on to serve him with some distinction yourself. I have heard it said that many a great man took his trusted Coxswain ashore with him when he retired to some great house. When you see him next, you can tell him that a 'fortune teller' told you that a knighthood will be expected very soon."

Howard looked up for just a moment and said:

"Oh aye, an ah wad no be expectin anythin less!"

He dropped me off along the shore just below the folly and I gave him one of the Captain's guineas. For some frightened moment I looked up to see that the folly was still there, then relaxed remembering that it was still there back even in my own time.

I quickly scrambled up the hill and looked around as I approached the folly. There was no one in sight, so I entered and looked for the pieces of my apparatus. To my great relief, the sections of my Faraday Cage were still leaning up against the wall, now slightly rusty after the months which I had spent at sea. My wooden base and stool had remained hidden high up in the folly and I reached up into the hidden alcove with trembling fingers to retrieve the all-important handset. It was still there wrapped in its protective covering of twentieth-century plastic and gaffer tape. I took out my diary and placed it back into the secret alcove along with the envelope which contained my discharge papers and the captain's orders.

I saw no reason for any more delay but I took one look at old Plymouth town across the bay and the small frigate sitting prettily across the water. I assembled my Faraday Cage and climbed in, securing the last panel home. I sat down on the wooden stool and carefully adjusted the controls on the handset. Luckily, the first thing which I had written in my diary after purchasing it, was the exact date, day and time when I had originally left my own time. I dialled the handset to that time and added five minutes just to be sure. I put on my goggles and pressed the main button. There was the comforting bright blue flash and my journey back to the future had started.

"What ho, Old Fruit! You're back!" came the excited cry from Fitzy who had climbed up into the folly when he saw the blue flash. "My God!" he continued. "You do look a fright!"

I suppose that a man returning from two hundred years in the past should have changed a little even if for me it was only two months. My nice set of theatrical eighteen-century clothes were dishevelled, dirty and torn in places and Fitzy was quick to point out that there were now flecks of grey in what was once my jet-black hair.

"Let's pack up and go home." I said with that exhaustion one gets when coming through some major trial. Then I remembered several important matters for Fitzy's benefit.

"Oh, search up there in the high wall of the folly. You will find some papers and a tarred package containing a rather full diary of several months at sea with the Royal Navy. I'll explain on the way home. Oh, and was there ever a FitzAdam in the navy?" I asked.

"Oh, you mean 'The Admiral'?" he replied with some flippancy. "He was apparently in the wars of that time as a Middie and went on to be an admiral in the Crimea. Crusty old salt, I'm told by my cousin Bertie who is descended from him. It was some of Bertie's tales when I was just a lad of the old boy's exploits that got me interested in the lives of sailors of his time."

"Well." I said "I strongly advise you to see old Bertie ASAP and look for his ancestor's diary. It will match the diary I have made for you and you may even find some reference to 'Landsman Jenkins' in it. We got to be good friends.

"Right oh, then." said Fitzy. "But why did you not bring the diary back with you in your jolly old birdcage?"

"Sometimes you are a silly clot, FitzAdam! How could you use a diary in your research which it is as new-looking as one purchased in the High Street yesterday? Take care when you open that package though, and especially the envelopes because now they have all aged for two hundred years! Your Prof. can do carbon dating on them and then he will find that they date back to 1796 and not 1996. You should also have some original artefacts now with these other documents – hand-written by myself as Captains Clerk I might add – and the two diaries. You can finish your Doctorate now, I hope."

We loaded up all of my apparatus into the old Landrover and headed off back home. It had been only five minutes of Fitzy's time but a long few months for me and two hundred years of history.

Time to go home.

Epilogue

It had been several months now since Fitzy and I had returned from the folly and my return from two hundred years in the past. I had packed my apparatus and experimental details away in a very tight storage box and put it into the Faculty's storage. Now I tried to put it all aside by getting back to my previous task of writing up the work which had led to my unsuccessful experiments with sub-atomic particles. They were mostly mathematical and suggestive of future research – all theoretical of course and I also had some letters to attend to.

I thought that even if the Faculty of Physics and the general scientific community had accepted my experiments on time travel, the world was probably not yet ready for such voyages. I often had dreams of the sort of abuse that could arise with unscrupulous people going back in time and altering the well-known history which school masters liked to dish out in lessons and those found in books. It was more frightening to think about going into the future and learning of horrible fates which might await us or our loved ones. For one, I much preferred to wait it out and enjoy the time given to me.

I was sitting in what was now a very sparsely furnished laboratory when Fitzy once again opened the door without knocking and put his head around the corner.

"What oh, Old Fruit! Time for a pint. Come and meet my cousin from Lowestoft."

I had just finished reading an acceptance letter from one of the prestigious universities in Australia which had offered me an Associate Professor's position in Particle Physics based on my previous papers. Naturally I was in a very happy mood and a pint was just what was needed, even if it was to be in the company of one of Fitzy's boring cousins. Wodehouse would have had a wealth of research material for his books using Fitzy's family tree and those who fell out of it.

To say that I was stunned when I went through my laboratory door and came face to face with Fitzy's 'boring cousin' would be a great understatement. I stood transfixed for what was probably a long time for a time traveller, for there in front of me was my lost girl from the past; the girl with the hazel eyes.

"This is my cousin Andrea," said Fitzy in a noncommittal way.

I was still lost for words but eventually took my gaze from her face and looked at Fitzy with some shock on my face. I turned once more to the beautiful girl and was barely able to mutter:

"Ummm... I suppose you might like to join us in a pint," I said without much class. She looked at me and gave me that same enigmatic smile which I had remembered from that time past:

"As you so desire, young sir," she said with a little laugh and a twinkle in her lovely hazel eyes.

Nautical Terms Explained

AB or 'Able Bodied', a term even used today for professional sailors skilled in seamanship.

Andrew (the) – sailor slang for the Royal Navy, probably derived from a man called Andrew Miller, a zealous officer of the Impress Service during the French Revolutionary and Napoleonic Wars. Miller 'recruited' so many men to His Majesty's ships that the navy was said to belong to him.

Bargemen – slang term for weevils or maggots which often inhabited ship's biscuit as they looked like 'crew' on board the flat, barge-like bread.

Bedlam – not specifically a naval word but referring to Bethlehem Royal Hospital, also known as St Mary Bethlehem, Bethlehem Hospital and often referred to as Bedlam. It is a psychiatric hospital in London founded in 1247 but moved a short distance to Moorfields in 1676 and now is located in Monks Orchard.

Berth (sailors') – refers to a sailor's sleeping area or his position on board a ship.

Bilge – physically refers to the lowest part of a ship's hull which collects dirty water but here used as a slang term for rubbish or nonsense e.g. 'that's no bilge, mate!'

Billets – living quarters on board a ship or barracks.

Boatswain (or Bos'n) - Petty Officer who is the senior most hand on deck and is responsible for the components of a ship's hull.

Boatswain's (Bos'n's) call is the small metal whistle used on naval ships to 'pipe' or blow signals for action on board ship.

Bollards – vertical metal or wooden stubby posts on ships or wharves used for tying the ship securely.

Bowsprit – the long, protruding spar at the front of a ship.

Buntlines - one of several lines fastened to the foot of a square sail at its middle for hauling it up to the yard when furling or typing it to the yard.

Capstan - is a vertical-axled rotating machine developed for use on sailing ships, usually to control the anchor, and is similar to that of a windlass, which has a horizontal axle.

Cathead - a horizontal beam extending from each side of a ship's bow, used for raising and carrying an anchor.

Clewlines - are lines (ropes) used to handle the corner of sails of a square-rigged ship.

Deckhead - is the underside of a deck of a ship it forms the ceiling of the cabins below.

Discharge – here refers to a sailor leaving his ship. They could be 'Honourable' or 'Dishonourable' or DD – 'Discharged Dead' if killed in battle.

Dog Watch – these were two watches of only two-hour duration between the hours of 1600 -1800 Hours (4pm to 6pm) and 1800 to 2000 Hours (8pm). These broke up the rosters of the Watch so that crews did not score the same Watch every day. The term may come from the hours at which 'even a dog should be asleep' or in reference of the first appearance of Sirius, the 'Dog Star' (in the constellation of Canis Major - the Great Dog).

Dons – sailor's term for their Spanish counterparts, probably derived from the honorific word used when referring to important Spanish men.

East Indiaman - was a general name for any sailing ship operating under charter or licence to any of the East India trading companies of the major European trading powers of the 17th through the 19th centuries, especially the Honourable East India Company of Great Britain.

Eye of the Wind - the direction from which the wind is blowing.

Fish Tackle – here it refers to the lines and pulleys used to secure (or 'fish') the anchor to the cathead.

Frigate - In the 18th century, a frigate was any warship built for speed and manoeuvrability. These carried guns on a single deck or on two decks (with further smaller guns usually carried on the forecastle and quarterdeck of the vessel).

Furl – the act of bundling and securing the sails to the yards when they are not in use.

Futtock Shrouds - are rope, wire or chain lines ('shrouds') which run from the outer edges of a top (platform on top of a mast) downwards and inwards to a point on the mast or lower shrouds and prevent any tendency of the top itself to tilt relative to the mast.

Gaskets – small lengths of rope which are used to tie a sail onto the yardarm when the sails are furled.

Grog – watered-down rum served to sailors probably after 1770. The word probably came from the habit of British Vice-Admiral Edward Vernon who gave this unpopular order and who often wore a coat of grogram cloth (a coarse, loosely woven fabric of silk and mohair) and who was nicknamed *Old Grogram* or *Old Grog*.

Gunwale (gunnel or gun'le) - the upper edge of the side of a vessel.

Halyards – is a line (rope) used to hoist or turn a yard (yardarm) – the cross-pieces of timber on a mast of a square-rigged ship. The term comes from the phrase, 'to haul yards' and form part of the 'running (moveable) rigging' of a ship.

Hard Tack – ship's bread or biscuit which was usually 'thrice-baked' to help its preservation over time. Usually very hard and often contained weevils or maggots. The term 'tack' was another sailor slang for 'food'.

Hove to – a term meaning that the ship has purposely stopped in the water by backing and probably lowering their sails. Anchors may be dropped if the water was shallow.

Idlers – those important persons on board who, because of their occupations, did not keep Watch such as the Cook, Sailmaker, Carpenter etc.

Jibs – triangular sails usually tied ('bent') on at the bow (front) of the ship.

Jolly Boat - was a type of ship's boat used mainly to ferry personnel to and from the ship, or for other small-scale activities.

Larboard – the port side or the left-hand-side of a vessel when facing its front or bow. This term comes from Middle English *ladebord* referring to the side on which the cargo or load (*lade*) was carried on board.

Because it was too similar to the term *starboard*, the Royal Navy ordered that *port* be used instead.

Lobscouse - type of (Norwegian) stew, typically made from chunks of meat, potatoes and onion and any other vegetable at hand. It was popular with sailors and is particularly associated with the port of Liverpool, which is why the inhabitants of that city are often referred to as 'scousers'.

Loblolly Boys - is the informal name given to the assistants to a ship's Surgeon aboard British warships during the Age of Sail. The name derives from a porridge traditionally served to sick or injured crew members.

Master-at-Arms - is a ship's senior rating, normally carrying the rank of Chief Petty Officer or Warrant Officer who is in charge of discipline aboard ship.

Mess Cooks – here refers to the normal members of a ship's mess, the small group who eat together, who on a rostered system go to the ships Galley (kitchen) to bring back the food items for the rest of their mess.

Neaters – usually refers to 'neat' or undiluted rum as opposed to 'grog' which was watered down.

Sailors always had a way of obtaining the 'real stuff' and often had a bottle 'stashed away'.

Neatsfoot Oil - is a yellow oil rendered and purified from the shin bones of cattle ('neat' comes from an Old English word for cattle). It is used as a conditioning, softening and preservative agent for leather and timber.

Paid Off - refers to the end of a cruise for sailors or even a ship. This was the time when the crew were paid their wages and could go ashore.

Pawl - each of a set of short bars that engage with the raised notches or strips on a capstan and prevent it from recoiling.

Pipe Down - whistled signal given to crews via a Boatswain's pipe meaning 'time to go below decks and retire for the evening,' or 'be quiet as it's time for lights out'.

Post Captains - in the Royal Navy of the 18th and 19th centuries, an officer might be promoted from commander to captain, but not have a command. Until the officer obtained a command, he was 'on the beach' and on half-pay. An officer 'took post' or was 'made post' when he was first commissioned to command a vessel. The term is now obsolete.

Powder Monkey – term for a crewman, usually a young boy, who was responsible to fetching the powder charges from the ship's magazine.

Press Gangs – were groups of sailors from the Impress Service or off a specific ship who went to dockside taverns and other places where seaman might congregate with the task of taking them onto ships of the Royal Navy. Thus, the men were said to be 'pressed'. This was often done by force as opposed to Volunteers who would accept the 'Kings Shilling' as an initial payment to go aboard.

Protections – documents issued to sailors which would 'protect' them from being 'pressed'. These were often also issued to persons with important occupations ashore as well as to prime seamen engaged on vital merchant ships.

Purser ('Pusser') – with the Rank of Warrant Officer, he is the person principally responsible for the purchasing and handling of money and stores and the administration of such items on board.

Quartermaster – a Petty Officer with particular responsibility for steering and signals as well as looking after stores.

Quoin – the wedge placed under the rear end of a muzzle-loading cannon. By pushing it in or out, the gun muzzle could be raised or lowered.

Ratlines (rattlin's) - are lengths of thin line tied between the shrouds of a sailing ship to form a ladder up each side of a mast and connecting the gunwales to each mast top.

'Runners' – deserters from the ship. To 'run' was a serious offence.

'Salt Junk' – the sailor's term for salt meat, usually beef or pork which would have been kept salted in barrels for months or years.

'Scran' - is a Scottish word used often by sailors meaning provisions or food. Sometimes used as a term for a meal, such as "What's for scran, mate?"

Scuttlebutt – ships gossip and general news as in 'on the grapevine' for landsmen. Derived probably by exchanged gossip when sailors went to the deck water cask, a wooden barrel or 'butt' which had been 'scuttled' (wreaked) by putting a hole in it from which the water could be obtained.

Scrimshaw - is scrollwork, engravings, and carvings done in bone or ivory. More commonly known as a hobby of Whalers, it was also common amongst other sailors.

'Sea Lawyer' - a sailor inclined who often questions or complains about the orders given or conditions on board the ship.

Shako – general Marine and Army conical hat with a peak.

Shanty (Sea) – seaman's work songs, often sung when a group was doing some task such as Halyard Shanties in hauling the yards or a Capstan Shanty in raising the anchor. Usually there was a 'shanty man' who sang the main verse followed by a chorus from the others.

Sheets – general nautical term for 'ropes'. The only rope on board called as such is that attached as the bell rope.

Shrouds – or lines of steel cable or stout rope holding the masts. Also used in the modern sense as a burial sheet.

'Sippers' – slang term for a drink (usually rum) from someone else, usually as a favour or kind of currency. 'Gulpers' were those who over did their proffered amount and 'Sandy Bottoms' were uncouth types who drank the lot!

'Slush' – the fatty material which floated to the surface when the ships 'salt tack' (beef or pork) was boiled in the Cook's stove. Cook would often sell this item to the rest of the crew to be used for various purposes, mainly as a spread. This is why the nickname for a cook was 'Slushy'.

Small Beer – low alcoholic beer used with grog and wine as the preferred drink on board as the water often was foul.

Standing Rigging – those fixed cables which never moved on a ship but usually held masts and other fittings in place. The shrouds with their ratlines where standing rigging.

Starboard – the right-hand-side of a ship when facing the front. The term probably comes from that derived from the Old English *steorbord*, meaning the side on which the ship is steered. Before ships had rudders on their centrelines, they were steered with a steering oar at the stern of the ship on the right-hand side of the ship, because more people are right-handed.

Stern – the back end of a ship as opposed to the stem or bow or front of a ship.

Swab – sailor's term for a useless or contemptible person, often in reference to a new 'wet' hand. Also used for the wet rope, rag or sponge pushed down the gun barrel or used on a pole to 'swab' or clean the decks.

Taffrail - a rail and ornamentation round a ship's stern.

Tar – more commonly 'Jack Tar' as a name for the common sailor. Also, another name for pitch which was used in water-proof cloth, rope and timber e.g. 'tarpaulin', a sailor's tar-coated jacket and another name given to common sailors.

Tell-tails (or **tell-tale**), is a piece of yarn or fabric attached to a sail or standing rigging to indicate the wind direction or flow of air over the sail.

Topmen – agile sailors who specialised in going aloft and handling the upper sails and rigging as opposed to 'deckmen' who did similar work whilst on deck. Considered the elite job on board.

Watch – the act of keeping a lookout and also the name for the group of men who work together and also 'keep watch' on a rostered system over twenty-four hours. The watches on board ship are:

Watch	Time
First Watch	2000–0000
Middle Watch	0000–0400
Morning Watch	0400–0800
Forenoon Watch	0800-1200
Afternoon Watch	1200–1600
First Dog Watch	1600–1800
Second Dog Watch	1800–2000

'Wet' – sailor's term for having a drink.

Yardarm – the outer extremity of a ships **yards** which hold the sails on a square-rigged ship,

About the Author

Dr. Scott on the bowsprit of the Brigantine *One-and-All*, Hamilton Island, Queensland.

Dr. Peter Terence Scott was born in Sydney, Australia and had a professional teaching career spanning over forty years, many of which was in teaching Physics. He studied part-time at university, obtaining a Bachelor's then a Masters' Degree in Science, a Masters' Degree in Educational Administration and later a Doctorate in Education. He also was an Army Reserve Officer and an Officer/Instructor in the Australian Naval Cadets for twelve years and Captain of Training Ship *Magnus*. Loving the old-fashioned life at sea he signed on for six training cruises on 'Tall Ships', both square-rigged and schooner -rigged. He has travelled to all six continents, including sailing down the Antarctic Peninsula and the Australian Great Barrier Reef. Now retired, he lives in Brisbane, Australia with his family and writes novels.

Other Books by the Author

FICTION

Letters from San Rafael (as Hernan Moreno Ruiz). Set in South America in the 1880's, this is a collection of letters smuggled home by Don Hernan Moreno, an Intelligence officer of the Peruvian Army who has been captured by the Ecuadorans during a border dispute. Taken to the fortified hacienda in Banos, in the mountains of Ecudor, he and his sargeant, Garcia, are treated as honoured guests. Each of the ten stories tells of the life and times of people in the hacienda and beyond. The final chapter is the climax of the entire book.

Return to San Rafael is the sequel to **Letters from San Rafael**. It is now 1891 and it has been five years since Colonel Moreno and his faithful sergeant Garcia had escaped San Rafael. Now, Moreno receives a mysterious coded letter asking them to return to San Rafael to solve its secret and ensure the stability of both Ecuador and Peru.

The Ice Ship. Set mainly in the Antarctic in the 1840's, this is the story of the survival of the crew of the futuristic auxiliary steam whaler, the *AUSTRALIS* which has become trapped in the ice following its voyage south along the Antarctic Peninsula. Based upon actual observations and experience of the author during a 2011 voyage into the same region on a small ex-research vessel.

The Innocence of Tom Shipley is the first novel

about young teacher Tom Shipley. It begins during his days at High School and his penchant as a Laboratory Prefect in making explosives and other prankish devices, follows him through similar acts at Teachers College and then out into his first appointment at age nineteen into the profession of teaching. At a brand-new school in Canberra, he finds that as the sole Science teacher, he is now the Acting Head of Department charged with establishing this subject at the school and equipping and managing several laboratories and new incoming staff. **A 'must read' for all teachers and parents.**

Tom Shipley's War, a sequel to the **Innocence of Tom Shipley** is about the young man's protest against those who protested about National Servicemen who were called up for the Vietnam War. He volunteers for the local Citizens' Military Forces unit (later the Army Reserve) and finds another war entirely: one with the more conservative members of the Army who still believe in WW2 tactics. Based on the author's own experiences as a young officer.

NON-FICTION

Adventures in Earth Science is an in-depth, traditional Earth Science textbook on Geology, Meteorology, Oceanography and Astronomy.

The latestscientific information has been given in the text including chapters on climate change and the future use of fuels and energy. The book contains over 700 pages, 1200 photographs and illustrations mostly taken by the author. It also includes 32 video links taken by the author to explain various skills as well as excursions to many exotic places in support of the text. Also has companion **Teachers' Guide** and **Laboratory Manual**.

The contents of this book have also been rearranged into the **Adventures in Earth Science Series** of eight smaller individual books in both electronic and A5 print editions.

Exploration Science

Fossils- Life in the Rocks

Riches from the Earth

A Dangerous Planet: Volcanoes & Earthquakes

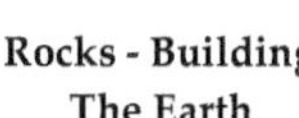

Rocks - Building The Earth

Changing the Surface: Weathering & Erosion

Through Sea & Sky: Oceanography/ meteorology

Beyond Planet Earth: Astronomy

Adventures in Earth and Environmental Science is a two-volume textbook on the environment, how it is monitored and implications for the future. They come in electronic format and as A4-sized print editions with a **Laboratory Manual** for each volume and a **Teachers' Guide**.

Surviving Global Warming - A Guide for the Future is

a comprehensive explanation of the natural and man-made causes of global warming with data from a wide range of reputable scientific bodies such as CSIRO and NASA. Written with many innovative suggestions for coping with the consequences of future global warming at the home, local and government levels. It comes as an electronic or printed edition.

A Pocketbook for Hiking and Survival is a concise reference book on going into the wild places of the Earth based on the author's extensive experience as a hiker, caver, geologist, Infantry Officer, ski instructor and leader of several youth groups. Topics include basic equipment, food, water, shelter, rope work, navigation and communications. The book is designed to be carried in pocket or backpack to where mobile phone signals may be lost. It is available in Kindle format as well as paperback and it is recommended that mobile phone users install it as a stand-alone document.

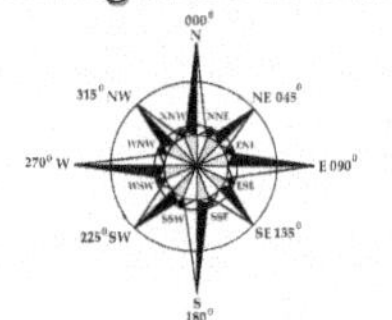

A Pocketbook for Surviving Teaching & Instruction is NOT an academic text on Education, but rather a sometimes-light-hearted guide to the art of teaching with some asides for instructors in the corporate or industrial world. It is written in a simple, easy-to-understand manner and so would be suitable for parents wishing to know more about the

teaching profession, especially if they are involved in home schooling. The text has been illustrated with some of the author's cartoons with a chapter on the use of such art in the classroom.

All of these books are available in electronic format for any PC or tablet in Kindle format which can be read on any device using the free Kindle App. Or as print editions. Available at all Internet book outlets or from **Felix Publishing** by contacting them at:

info.felixpublishing@gmail.com

www.ingramcontent.com/pod-product-compliance
Lightning Source LLC
Chambersburg PA
CBHW070629170726
48291CB00003B/933